LAKE OF BONES

A James Acton Thriller

Also by J. Robert Kennedy

James Acton Thrillers

The Protocol	*Blood Relics*	*The Cylon Curse*
Brass Monkey	*Sins of the Titanic*	*The Viking Deception*
Broken Dove	*Saint Peter's Soldiers*	*Keepers of the Lost Ark*
The Templar's Relic	*The Thirteenth Legion*	*The Tomb of Genghis Khan*
Flags of Sin	*Raging Sun*	*The Manila Deception*
The Arab Fall	*Wages of Sin*	*The Fourth Bible*
The Circle of Eight	*Wrath of the Gods*	*Embassy of the Empire*
The Venice Code	*The Templar's Revenge*	*Armageddon*
Pompeii's Ghosts	*The Nazi's Engineer*	*No Good Deed*
Amazon Burning	*Atlantis Lost*	*The Last Soviet*
The Riddle		*Lake of Bones*

Special Agent Dylan Kane Thrillers

Rogue Operator	*Black Widow*	*State Sanctioned*
Containment Failure	*The Agenda*	*Extraordinary Rendition*
Cold Warriors	*Retribution*	*Red Eagle*
Death to America		*The Messenger*

Templar Detective Thrillers

The Templar Detective	*The Sergeant's Secret*	*The Black Scourge*
The Parisian Adulteress	*The Unholy Exorcist*	*The Lost Children*
	The Code Breaker	

Kriminalinspektor Wolfgang Vogel Mysteries

The Colonel's Wife	*Sins of the Child*

Delta Force Unleashed Thrillers

Payback	*The Lazarus Moment*	*The Cuban Incident*
Infidels	*Kill Chain*	*Rampage*
	Forgotten	

Detective Shakespeare Mysteries

Depraved Difference	*Tick Tock*	*The Redeemer*

Zander Varga, Vampire Detective

The Turned

LAKE OF BONES

A James Acton Thriller

J. ROBERT KENNEDY

Copyright ©2022 J. Robert Kennedy

ISBN: 9781990418242

First Edition

For Jim Dunn, a good friend to the family.

You will be missed.

LAKE OF BONES

A James Acton Thriller

"Our country has never bowed down and will never bow down to any world power."

Indian Prime Minister Narendra Modi after a border clash between Indian and Chinese troops
July 3, 2020

"Over the past year-and-a-half, the India-China bilateral relationship has deteriorated like never before and it will continue to deteriorate further. So the country has to be prepared for the change that is coming."

Gautam Bambawale, former Indian Ambassador to China
October 2021

PREFACE

On June 15, 2020, an outrageous border incident occurred where Chinese and Indian troops were involved in a melee near the Galwan River. No shots were fired, however reports indicate Chinese troops that had previously crossed the border, set upon an Indian patrol with iron rods, clubs, and batons wrapped in barbed wire. The hand-to-hand combat took place in the pitch dark and lasted over six hours before reinforcements arrived from the Indian side. The battle eventually involved over 600 soldiers, some of whom were tossed in the fast-flowing river, leading to their deaths.

The final toll is disputed, however it is believed the Chinese lost 43 troops and the Indians 20. Prisoners were taken by both sides, though were quickly released after de-escalation meetings.

This was all triggered by the Indians building a road on their side of the border, in undisputed land, likely because it would allow the Indians to respond quickly to any Chinese incursions. Over the decades, there have been many incidents in this region, including all-out war. The area is a powder keg waiting for one more match to be struck, and the belligerent Chinese show no signs of backing down.

China is challenging the world not only in this region, but in the South China Sea, Taiwan, Hong Kong, and more. Eventually, they will cross a line that the nations of the world cannot ignore, when China overreacts to yet another threat perceived only by themselves.

Perhaps today is that day.

Indian Army Northern Command Communications Center

Uttarakhand, India

Present Day

Interpol Agent Hugh Reading gripped Laura Palmer's hand as they rushed down the steps. An alarm blared behind them indicating what they had feared had now begun. War had broken out, and everyone inside the new state-of-the-art communications facility built on the Indian side of the border with China, only had minutes to live. The man he was proud to call one of his best friends, if not his best friend, hailed them as he rushed from another door. James Acton was probably the bravest man he had ever met, and his wife Laura by far the bravest woman. They were the best of people, and he had to save them somehow.

His eyes scanned for a solution. The parking lot was overflowing with vehicles, both military and civilian, here for the opening ceremony. Acton had gone to find their driver but had returned alone, which meant he had been unsuccessful, and if Chinese cruise missiles were inbound, there was no time to find another vehicle. They would have to make a run for it, though there was no way he'd be fast enough.

He wasn't surviving this, but his younger friends still could.

He continued to search for a solution as his friends talked, then another problem introduced itself as the first of the guests inside rushed through the doors in a panic, racing toward the parked cars.

"Can we get far enough away on foot?" asked Laura.

Reading shook his head. "I can't, but you two might be able to." He grabbed them each by the arm, hugging them hard, then pointed toward the gate as he struggled to control his emotions. "Go now. Don't waste a moment. I'll try to get us a vehicle and pick you up."

"Bullshit to that!" protested his friend. "If you think for a second—"

"Look!" Laura pointed at the roof and they all turned to see Senator Simmons' chopper lifting off before banking away from the facility. "Thank God, Tommy and Mai are safe."

Reading pushed the two of them away. "And now it's time for you two to get safe. That's an order. Don't let your stubbornness get you killed. You sacrificed your seats to save them. Let me sacrifice myself to save you. Now go!"

Laura sobbed and grabbed him, holding him tight as Acton stared into his eyes, the pain his friend held back speaking volumes. Reading reached out and squeezed his friend's shoulder, his heart aching with the knowledge he would never see them or anyone he loved again.

"Tell Spencer I love him." His voice cracked at the mention of his son, and Acton gripped his hand.

"You can count on it." Acton pointed at the parking lot. "Steal a car if you have to. I expect to see you soon."

Reading watched as his friends sprinted down the road toward the gates. He wasn't certain what the blast radius would be nor how many missiles the Chinese might send at the complex, mostly buried inside the side of the mountain, but if they ran quickly, they stood a chance of surviving. Civilians in formal attire here for the opening ceremony rushed past him and he ignored them, instead beginning a slow walk toward the gate, never feeling so old as he did now.

Five years ago, he would have been running with his friends, but not anymore. His joints were too stiff, his muscles too sore, his Interpol desk job he had been relegated to after a long proud career at Scotland Yard, had killed him in a way he had never expected. At least the Chinese were putting him out of his misery. His only regret was that he wouldn't get a chance to say goodbye to his son, but at least he'd die knowing the others had survived.

Acton and Laura were nearing the gate now, and the helicopter carrying their young friends, Tommy and Mai, along with Senator Simmons who had got them into this mess, was almost out of sight. He stared at the lone chopper then scanned the skies for the second one that had been promised for him and the others.

And found nothing.

A massive explosion tore through the air. He spun to hear Laura scream and his jaw dropped at the sight of the helicopter carrying the oh-so innocent Tommy and Mai fall from the sky. He collapsed to his knees, his shoulders slumping as he lost all will to live, and begged God for the Chinese missiles to end his sorrow.

Outside Esztergom, Kingdom of Hungary

AD 1252

"Your mother was a heretic. The price for her entry into the Kingdom of Heaven will be steep."

Oldamur stared at Father Tamas. The man was new, not here a year, a replacement sent by Rome after the death of the village priest, the only man who had ever tended to Oldamur's religious needs. Father Miklos had been a good man, a caring man, a man who attended every birth, who conducted every funeral, every baptism, who knew every name in their small community.

But Tamas was different. While he couldn't expect to have the history, he didn't conduct himself in a manner Oldamur felt was required by a priest. Tamas showed no interest in learning their names, was gruff, and made no effort to proactively tend to the needs of his flock. He seemed more concerned with the tithe collection each Sunday, making it a point to mention whenever the previous week's donations were light.

Murmurs around the village among those who would dare gossip about their religious leader suggested others had noticed what he had— their new priest sent from Rome was more obsessed with money than with the spiritual wellbeing of those he was responsible for.

And this latest statement removed all doubt.

"She was *not* a heretic," he replied through clenched teeth.

"I don't recall seeing your mother at church in the entire time I've been here. And in speaking with others, they've informed me that she never attended services. If that's the case, then she hasn't confessed her sins, therefore she now suffers in purgatory, waiting for her family to attend to the matter."

Oldamur growled, pulling at his hair as he spun, his back now facing the frustrating man. He held his breath, calming himself lest he say something truly egregious. He exhaled. "Ask anyone in the village. My mother was a God-fearing woman, the kindest soul you could ever hope to meet."

"If she was a God-fearing woman, then why did she not attend church?"

Oldamur turned to face the rotund man, who likely hadn't put in a hard day's work in his entire life. "When she was a little girl, her father died helping build this very church. Coming here was simply too painful, so she and my aunts and uncles vowed never to set foot inside, and instead worshipped in their own way."

Tamas' eyebrows rose and he leaned forward on his desk, reaching for his pen and ink. "And the names of these aunts and uncles?"

Oldamur bristled. "Are irrelevant to this discussion as they are already dead."

"Then they too suffer in purgatory. Give me their names and I'll speak with their families to absolve them of their sins committed while they were alive."

"We're here to discuss my mother. You had one of your altar boys fetch me from the farm indicating it involved my mother's soul. Now you tell me a fee must be paid to the Church for you to grant an indulgence to forgive her for sins I'm certain God would have already forgiven her for, considering how minor they were."

"Sin is sin. And who are you to judge what God considers minor?"

Oldamur sighed. There was no point arguing the matter with the man. The Church said his mother was condemned, perhaps for eternity, to suffer in a state of purgatory, but there was the possibility he could free her from such a horror and gain her entry into Heaven if he purchased an indulgence. If there were a chance to save her, then it was his responsibility to do so, for Tamas was right—how could he know what God wanted? He was just a man who had lost his mother, and the spiritual guidance being given to him, no matter how he felt about the man providing it, was nothing he hadn't heard before.

He closed his eyes. "How much? How much will it take to ensure my mother gains entry into Heaven?"

"I've already prepared the indulgence. All it requires is my signature, and your mother's soul will be unburdened. I fear, however, the price will be steep."

When Oldamur heard the amount, he collapsed.

The Oval Office, The White House

Washington, D.C.

Present Day, Three Days Earlier

"Pardon my French, sir, but frankly, the Chinese are going apeshit over this."

The president grunted at Leif Morrison's assessment. The National Clandestine Service Chief of the CIA was an uncommonly blunt man, and Senator Joseph Simmons liked him for that very reason. The president's inner circle couched their advice in political terms, which far too often made a serious situation appear not so much so. There was no risk of that when Morrison was in the room—he could always be counted on to give the straight dirt.

The president turned to him. "Well, what do you think, Joe? Are the Chinese going 'apeshit' like Leif says?" Air quotes were delivered.

Simmons chuckled. "They are, sir. The question is whether it's for domestic consumption or if they actually mean to follow through. They are claiming the construction of the communications facility is a hostile act."

"It is," said Morrison. "If you believe the best offense is a good defense."

The president regarded him. "Isn't it usually the other way around?"

Morrison shrugged. "In my experience, it goes either way. Mr. President, we knew this was going to piss the Chinese off. Everything pisses the Chinese off, and if we continually give in to them, they'll quickly dominate the region. They have to be shown that what happens outside their borders is beyond their control. India setting up a communications facility near a border the Chinese have crossed on multiple occasions is only provocative because the Chinese choose to view it that way. The Indians have a right to secure their borders, and that facility will provide them with far superior communications capabilities in the region than they currently have. The Chinese don't like that if they did choose to invade, every corner of India would know immediately, negating some of the advantages they now have. It's too easy for them to jam communications under the current setup. This facility addresses that gap in their infrastructure. It's no different than the three centers the Chinese have on their side of the border."

An eyebrow shot up the president's forehead. "Three?"

Morrison shrugged. "Redundancies. Should the Indians take out one or two, they'll still have communications capability."

"And the Indians are only opening one?"

"The Chinese build under the presumption of war. Most of its neighbors don't."

"Perhaps they should," muttered Simmons.

"What was that, Joe?"

Simmons sighed. "I'm just so sick and tired of pussyfooting around the Chinese and the Russians. When the Cold War ended with the collapse of the Soviet Union, everyone kept talking about a peace dividend. The problem is, we've never had peace since. Instead of worrying about the Soviets, we had to contend with militant Islam, and now the Russians are almost as bad as they ever were, and the Chinese are far worse. God help us all if they can create an economy that can be sustained at current levels without Western consumers. They plan long term, and their intention is to control the world, not the small patch they currently have. This communications installation is of little importance strategically, but in their eyes, it's another domino that can't be allowed to fall."

The president pursed his lips and leaned back in his chair. "Then what would you propose?"

Morrison chimed in first. "I think we need to fly the flag."

Simmons eyed him. "Fly the flag?"

"Send someone there for the opening, someone high profile. The Chinese wouldn't dare take out the facility if an American delegation was there."

The president's head bobbed slowly. "I like the idea. But only a small delegation. We don't want to make it look like we're supporting them militarily by hogging the spotlight. Somebody important enough, though, that the Chinese would think twice before interfering."

Simmons liked the idea. "Did you have anybody in mind, Mr. President?"

He was answered with a broad smile. "How about yourself?"

Simmons' eyes shot wide. "It hadn't occurred to me, sir."

"You're the perfect choice. You're familiar with the file. You're a senator from the great state of Maryland. And most of all, I've known you for over twenty years. You're level-headed, and if the shit does hit the fan, as Leif might say, you've got fifteen years of military service under your belt."

"So, if the Chinese do decide to engage, you expect me to head them off singlehandedly?"

Everyone in the room laughed, including the Secretary of State, Daniel Hanks. "GI Joe. America's greatest hero."

Simmons shrugged. "Better than America's greatest zero, I suppose."

"When does this facility open again?" asked the president.

"Three days."

The president rose, followed immediately by the room. "Then, Senator, I do believe you and your wife have some packing to do."

Simmons bowed his head slightly, quickly formulating an excuse to keep his wife from harm's way. "Looking forward to doing my part, Mr. President. Unfortunately, my wife won't be able to attend as she's recovering from the flu."

"Understood. Send her my best."

"I will, sir. Thank you."

The room quickly emptied, and as Simmons headed to meet his driver, Morrison caught up to him. "I wonder if I might offer you a ride back to your office."

Simmons didn't bother letting the man know his own ride was waiting outside. Morrison only invited you into his car if he wanted to say something he didn't want overheard. "Thanks, that would be great."

Moments later, they were in the back of Morrison's car with the privacy shield up, though Simmons had little doubt the driver could be trusted implicitly.

"What did you want to talk to me about, Leif?"

"The little excursion I have no doubt you're already planning."

Simmons' eyebrows shot up. "Excuse me?"

"Every trip you go on, you take a side trip, either before or after."

"Yes, I suppose I do, depending on where I am. I am a bit of a—"

"Archaeology buff," interrupted Morrison. "Yes, we're all aware of it. This time, I highly recommend you reconsider."

Simmons regarded him. "Why? Do you really think the Chinese are going to try anything?"

"I can't say, but you heard the report this morning. The Chinese have amassed almost 200,000 troops at the border."

"But that's just saber-rattling."

"It could be, and I hope it is. Do I think the Chinese will invade and try to take India? Of course not. I don't even believe they'll invade and attempt to hold any territory. Much of what the Chinese do is for optics. If I were them, I would pour across that border, take the entire disputed region, hold it for a week, then pull out, just to prove it could be done and that there's nothing anybody could do to stop it. Then I'd begin negotiations."

"To what end?"

"Who knows? But I can guarantee you if they cross that border, that communications facility will be one of the first targets taken out, most likely before they cross."

"So then I shouldn't go."

Morrison shook his head. "No, the chances of them hitting the facility while you're in it are slim."

"I'm not exactly sure 'slim' fills me with confidence."

"Nor should it. My guess is the moment they know you're out of there, they'll hit it, or they'll hit it before you even get there."

"Why are you telling me this?"

"Because if something goes wrong, it's my job to protect you."

"I thought it was the job of the DSS?"

"That's your visible security. The Agency always has people in position, just in case."

"Well, I suppose that's comforting."

"It should be, Senator. Your security has to follow rules, mine doesn't. Now, are you still going on your side trip?"

Simmons pursed his lips for a moment. The only reason to not go would be to give in to fear of what the Chinese might be planning. And not doing things he loved to do, changing his plans because the enemy was using terror to affect his life, was something he had never done. Whether Chinese, Russians, North Koreans, or Islamic fundamentalists, he lived his life his way, the enemy be damned. He came to a decision.

15

"I'm afraid, Leif, you're not going to like my answer. If you've read my file, you know I never give in to terrorists, and that's all these Chinese are."

"Very well, Senator, there's nothing I can do to stop you. I assume you'll be inviting a subject matter expert?"

Simmons eyed him. "A what?"

"An archaeologist, or someone who can explain the location you plan to visit."

"Of course. I always try to bring along one of my constituents."

"So, someone from Maryland?"

"Of course. Our great state has experts in every field."

"Then might I make a suggestion?"

Outside Esztergom, Kingdom of Hungary

AD 1252

Oldamur bent down, removing the yoke from his shoulders, his entire body aching from his efforts to prepare the fields for planting. It was the most physically demanding part of his responsibilities, though it was also rewarding when done. It marked the beginning of another season and the promise of crops to sustain his family. The farm had been in his family for generations, and it was now his obligation to tend to it as the eldest surviving member.

Yet he was tortured. The conversation yesterday with Father Tamas still vexed him. If Tamas was correct, his mother would never enjoy what had been promised. She would suffer for eternity unless he could find a way to pay the exorbitant fee demanded by the Church for the required indulgence.

It made no sense to him. Why would God demand money for those who had sinned on Earth, to gain entry to Heaven? What use did God have for money? None. The Church had a need for it, but was the

Church God? It obviously wasn't, but the pope in Rome was chosen by God and was man's conduit to the Almighty. And surely, if God felt these indulgences weren't appropriate, He would have informed the pope.

Oldamur growled in frustration and his ox stamped his foot, reacting to his master's emotional state. It was all too frustrating, too maddening. If Father Miklos were alive, telling him the same thing, he would perhaps be more accepting as he would trust the messenger. And that was another thing that bothered him. His mother had died two days ago. How could Rome have set the price for her salvation? A message from here to Rome would take weeks just to arrive. It meant that Father Tamas had set the amount.

Yet how could he possibly fight it? Father Miklos would have set an amount within reason, something his family could hope to actually pay. The amount now demanded of them was unfathomable. Even if they sold all their crops for the next ten seasons, they couldn't hope to pay it. Not to mention the fact they would die from starvation. He could think of only one possible solution to save his mother's soul, but it was so unthinkable, it terrified him to even contemplate it, for it meant sacrificing everything, including his family's future.

He turned and watched his wife washing the clothes by the side of their humble home, their two children chasing a butterfly, giggling, blissfully oblivious to the problems of life as an adult. His hopes for them were simple. His son would grow up, marry, then one day take over the farm, his daughter would find a husband and move to his farm to raise their own children, and he and his wife would grow old and eventually pass, where they would reunite with lost loved ones and await the eventual arrival of their children and grandchildren.

Simple, uncomplicated. Work hard, be a good person, then be rewarded. But these indulgences changed everything. Now it was work hard, lead a good life, and hope your family's priest didn't decide you owed money for sins you may or may not have committed. It wasn't fair. It wasn't right.

A horse whinnied and he turned to see a group of people, perhaps a score, approaching along the road to the village, a mix of men, women, and children. A man atop the lone horse raised his hand, hailing him. "Greetings, good sir. May I have a word with you?"

The man's smile was pleasant, infectious even, especially with the foul mood Oldamur was in. He waved back. "Of course." He trudged through the freshly tilled fields, his wife joining him along with their children as the visitor made his way up in the lane that led to their house.

The man dismounted and extended a hand. "Good day. My name is Pierre Bellamy. Whom do I have the privilege of meeting today?"

"I'm Oldamur. This is my wife, Adelhaid, my son, Ajtony, and my daughter, Zaleska."

Pierre shook Oldamur's hand and bowed to the others. "A pleasure."

Oldamur regarded the ragtag group waiting on the road. "How can we help you, sir?"

Pierre extended an arm toward the others. "My friends and I are on a pilgrimage, and we're looking for a place to rest. I was hoping you might grant us permission to camp on your property for a couple of days. We, of course, don't expect to not do our part. I have able-bodied men and boys that will happily help you till your field and plant your crops in exchange for your hospitality."

Adelhaid took her husband's hand, staring up at him. "You could certainly use the help."

She was right. He could. The prospect of having others do the tilling was appealing. Incredibly appealing. But there was a problem. "I'm afraid we don't have enough food to feed so many."

The man smiled. "We are well provisioned. In fact, let us feed you."

"Oh, that's not necessary," protested Adelhaid.

Pierre smiled at her. "It's not necessary, which is why it would be our joy if you would accept the invitation."

Oldamur bowed his head. "We would be honored." He pointed to an area of the farm where the field was left to fallow for the season. "Your people can camp there. There should be enough room."

Pierre turned toward where Oldamur was pointing and his head bobbed, clearly pleased. "That will do perfectly. Thank you." He whistled and waved to those on the road, shouting something in a strange tongue that Oldamur had never heard before. Several others issued instructions, including one in his language, suggesting these people were from many lands. The group slowly made their way up the lane and over to the untended pasture, and Oldamur watched with his family as they set up camp.

Pierre noticed their awe. "Impressive, isn't it?"

"Indeed."

"Many of them have been doing this for months, and those that have just joined us will be as practiced as the others in short order. They'll teach those who have yet to join us."

Oldamur's eyes narrowed as he turned to face the man. "Just who are you people?"

Pierre patted him on the arm. "All will be explained when we share a meal together tonight."

Acton/Palmer Residence

St. Paul, Maryland

Present Day

Archaeology Professor James Acton held the stretch, the fingers of both hands touching the toes on his right foot. He rose and leaned back, stretching his arms high over his head and groaned in relief. "Ugh, I hate physiotherapy."

His wife, Archaeology Professor Laura Palmer, gave him a look. "You may hate it, but it's the only reason you're fully recovered from what happened in Germany."

He was about to sit beside her when she gave him the stink eye and pointed at the bath towel folded neatly on the table. He grabbed it and threw it on the couch before sitting. "Want to make out? I hear that's good for recovery from grenades."

"You're all sweaty and stinky."

His eyebrows bobbed suggestively. "I know, that's what makes it dirty."

"I don't think that's the kind of dirty they had in mind."

He pouted. "You're no fun."

"Go take a shower then we can have some fun."

The eyebrows bobbed again. "Or you could join me in the shower."

She patted his cheek. "We've tried that. It's too tight a squeeze to be fun."

Acton pointed at the tablet sitting on the table showing a real estate listing. "When we buy our new house, the master bath has to have a shower big enough to shag in."

She giggled. "You're terrible."

"Which is why you love me." He pushed to his feet. "Okay, I'm going to go and get un-dirty so you and I can get really dirty."

She tapped her watch. "Don't forget, Tommy and Mai are going to be here in an hour. And remember, you have to pack for our trip."

"We're going to Spain to lie on a beach. I plan on bringing two T-shirts, four thongs, and a pair of flip-flops."

She eyed him. "I'll give you a million dollars if you wear nothing but a thong the entire trip."

"You're going to regret that."

She groaned. "I knew the moment it came out of my mouth I would."

He smacked his ass. "What? You don't think I've got a spectacular butt?"

"You have the finest butt I've ever seen on an archaeologist."

He grinned then his smile collapsed. "Hey, wait a minute, that's a pretty narrow field."

She shrugged. "It doesn't make it a lie."

"Yes, it does."

Her eyes narrowed. "How so?"

"Because you're an archaeologist too, and"—he reached forward and grabbed her butt—"I've seen your ass. It's way nicer than mine."

She swatted his chest as he leaned in for a kiss. "You really do stink."

He stood straight. "Fine. I'm getting in that shower, then there are no more excuses."

She again tapped her watch. "Tommy and Mai."

"I'll hurry."

"Take your time, you might miss a spot. I promise when they head home, there will be plenty of time for snogging."

He groaned. "Great, now I'm going to be thinking about it all evening."

"There are worse things you could be thinking about."

"True, but now I have to wear pants and it's warm out."

She eyed him. "Why would you have to wear pants?"

He thrust his pelvis toward her. "Because shorts kind of reveal the beast."

She looked down then laughed. "Maybe I better join you in that shower."

He threw both hands up in the air. "Victory!" His phone rang and he cursed, picking it up off the table. He didn't recognize the number, and for a moment debated whether to take it.

"Who is it?"

"I don't know. Area code's DC, though." He swiped his thumb across the screen. "Hello?"

"Hello, this is Holly Davis from Senator Simmons' office. Am I speaking with Professor James Acton?"

"You are."

"Professor Acton, I'm calling on behalf of the senator. He's heading to India to attend the opening of a new facility there, and afterward, he wishes to visit an archaeological site. I believe it's called Skeleton Lake."

Acton's interest was piqued. "Skeleton Lake? That's a little out of the way, isn't it?"

"The fact you know that, Professor, means you know far more than I do, which is exactly why the senator would like to extend the invitation to you to act as his guide. It would only be for three days."

"And when would this be?"

"You would depart in two days."

Acton pursed his lips. "We have vacation plans with several others that begin in two days."

"Is there any way you could reschedule? The senator is very eager to visit this site, and you came highly recommended."

"Could you hold on for a moment?"

"Absolutely."

He pressed the phone to his chest. "Senator Simmons has asked that I accompany him to India, where after some event, he wants to visit Skeleton Lake."

Laura's face brightened. "Ooh, I'd love to see that."

Acton stuck his tongue out at her. "You weren't invited."

She pouted. "Did I hear you say this is in two days?"

25

"Yes. Unfortunate timing, but it's not often a senator makes a request of you."

"True. But Hugh and the others will be very disappointed."

"Well, Tommy and Mai can still go, and we can join them later."

Laura pursed her lips. "What about Hugh?"

"If *you* asked him to delay a few days, I doubt he'd mind."

"What if we brought him with us?" she suggested.

He liked the idea. "Maybe we can bring them all with us. Instead of lying on a beach in Spain, we can visit India and see the sights."

Laura concurred eagerly, pointing at the phone. "Ask them."

Acton returned the phone to his ear. "Sorry about that. I had to discuss things with my wife. Would it be possible for me to bring my wife, who is also an expert on Skeleton Lake, along with three of our friends that were supposed to be vacationing with us?"

"I'll have to check. Normally, we only allow one person to accompany an invitee."

"We'll take care of our own travel arrangements and expenses. We just need to know where and when to meet the senator."

"Five people, did you say?"

"Including me."

"I'm sure that can be arranged, especially if you're covering your own travel expenses. Let me get back to you to confirm it."

"No problem. Why don't you text me an email address so I can send you the names and contact details of those we'd like to bring with us, just to expedite things, as I'm sure your people will want to vet them."

"That's good thinking, Professor. I get the impression you've been through this before."

Acton chuckled. "You could say that."

The call ended and Laura stared up at him expectantly. "Well?"

"She's going to see if it's okay then call us back. Tommy shouldn't be a problem because he's a red-blooded American. You and Hugh will probably be fine as well because you're British citizens. We like you at the moment."

"You think Mai might be a problem?"

"She's got her citizenship, so she'd be able to fly with us, but because she was a Vietnamese citizen who left the country in a bit of a rush—"

"That's one way of putting it."

"—the senator's security might have concerns."

"Well, there's no way we're going to leave her behind. We all go, or none of us go. Or just you go."

He shook his head. "Hells no! You want to see Skeleton Lake as much as I want to see it. You're right, we all go or none of us go." His phone buzzed with a message from the senator's office providing the email address he had requested. He handed Laura the phone. "Do you mind taking care of this? I'm going to hit the showers."

She sighed, her shoulders slumping. "Sure. Now that you're going to get to see some mysterious archaeological site, you no longer need me to distract you."

He grabbed her by the hand and hauled her to her feet. "You can text from the shower. Just don't make any typos while I'm ravishing you."

27

Fairfax Towers
Falls Church, Virginia

CIA Analyst Supervisor Chris Leroux sat in a lawn chair on the roof of his apartment building. His girlfriend and CIA operations officer, Sherrie White, lay on a lounge chair next to him, enjoying the sun beating down on her gorgeous body while he hid from it under a beach umbrella. He had never known that some tenants in the building had set up this oasis until Sherrie had moved in with him and had been invited to the rooftop by some horny young men, no doubt eager to see her in a bathing suit. They had been disappointed when he showed up with her, then stunned at the real-life Leonard and Penny couple.

He still couldn't get over the fact he was with a woman as incredible as her. She was stunning, but more than that, she was remarkably intelligent, very good at what she did for a living, and he never doubted she truly did love him. And though she had dragged him out of his shell, he wasn't entirely out, so enjoying the celestial body he had spent so much of his life avoiding, was not his comfort zone. Whenever she wanted to come to the roof, however, he always went with her. Not because he didn't trust her, but because he didn't trust every other man on the planet except for his best friend from high school, Dylan Kane. Kane was another CIA operative that lived in the building with his girlfriend, Lee Fang, who was supposed to be joining them. The door swung open behind them and Fang appeared.

Speak of the devil.

Sherrie removed her sunglasses and waved. "I was wondering when you'd get here."

"Sorry I'm late." Fang repositioned another lounge chair beside Sherrie. "Dylan called, so I was on the phone with him."

"Oh, that's nice. I guess it's not often he gets to make a call while on a mission."

"No, which is why I figured you could wait."

Sherrie laughed and jerked her thumb at Leroux. "If this one was skydiving and I called him, he'd wait to pull the cord before finishing the conversation."

Leroux grunted. "Shows what you know. I'd pull the cord to give us more time to talk."

Sherrie held up her hand. "See? Always thinking, this one is."

Fang dropped her baggy sweatpants and pulled her T-shirt off, revealing a two-piece bikini leaving little to the imagination. Leroux caught himself staring and even Sherrie ogled her up and down. The former Chinese Special Forces officer was ripped.

Sherrie whistled. "I would slaughter a small village to have those abs."

Fang flushed and sat on the lounge chair. "Like you don't have abs."

"Not like that."

Fang pointed at Sherrie's chest. "I'd trade these abs for those any day."

Sherrie grinned and looked up at Leroux in his chair. "So darling, which would you rather? Fang's abs or these tatas?"

Leroux tensed, recognizing the trap. He flashed a smile. "Darling, I've learned over the past few years that there's only one correct answer to that, and that is whatever you think I should prefer to have."

Sherrie burst out laughing, reaching up and patting his leg. "Good answer. You're definitely getting some tonight."

It was Leroux's turn to blush.

Fang laid down and let out a loud groan. "Don't talk about sex. Dylan's been gone a week and I don't know when he's getting back."

Leroux's phone vibrated and he picked it up off his lap. He cursed.

Sherrie looked up at him. "What is it?"

"It's the office. I need to go in."

"Right away?"

"Yeah, it's the Chief himself."

"Well, I guess you better get a move on."

He stood and stared down at the two women. "You two all right up here alone?"

Sherrie slid her sunglasses down the bridge of her nose, giving him a look. "You do know that we kill people for a living, right?"

Leroux shivered, a tingle racing up and down his spine at the both terrifying and titillating statement. It was easy to forget what their jobs were. He ran ops from a distance on a regular basis that saved lives and took lives, and Sherrie was what the public thought of as an agent, a spy trained to kill for her country, and he knew firsthand she had done so more times than he cared to count. He had also seen Fang in action, and she was a lethal weapon, though her past was mostly a mystery. What she had done on behalf of the Chinese government before she had been forced into exile was anybody's guess, and he certainly wasn't the one who was going to ask—he was just happy she was on their side now.

His phone vibrated with another message that turned out to be a news alert. He grunted. "Well, the world just found out what we've known for weeks."

"What's that?" asked Fang.

"That the Chinese have put almost 200,000 troops on the Indian border."

Fang swung into a seated position, her feet now on the fake grass, the mention of her former homeland causing concern. "Is that accurate?"

"I'm afraid so. The build-up's been going on for a couple of months, but they really ramped it up over the past few weeks."

"Why?"

Leroux chewed his cheek for a moment, trying to remember if the reason were classified or not. Finally, he remembered reading a New York Times report on the facility. "The Indians have built a state-of-the-art communications facility near the border with China. Most of the hardware was provided by American companies. The Chinese are pissed and they're saying that if the facility goes online, they're going to treat it as an act of war and take it out."

Fang sighed as her head slumped and she stared at her feet. "I don't understand my country anymore. I used to, but now that I've been exposed to the real world, I realize just how backward we are. The Chinese government takes everything as a provocation, everything as a threat. When are they going to learn that no one wants to invade them? The vast majority of the world just wants to live in peace."

"That's how dictatorships hold on to power," said Leroux. "They have to unite the people behind them by making them focus their attention on a common enemy, external to their borders, when instead, the real enemy is within. China, Russia, North Korea, Iran, they're all various forms of dictatorship. The lives of their citizens would be far better if they were democracies, but as long as they're led by people who tell them that their enemy is outside their borders and the only hope they have to keep them out is their current leadership, they have no future. Unfortunately, we're going to be dealing with these countries forever if they don't smarten up."

"China and India have gone to war before."

"Yes, and between the two of them, there are almost three billion people involved. About thirty-five percent of the world's population would be affected if a full-scale war broke out between the two of them, not to mention their neighbors that could get dragged into the conflict."

"And us." Sherrie sat up. "Do you think that's why you've been called in?"

Leroux shrugged. "Could be. My team has been monitoring the border." He held up his wrist and shook his watch. "I'd better be going."

Fang stood. "I'm not really in the mood to just lie here anymore."

Sherrie agreed. "Neither am I. How about we get changed and you meet me at our apartment? We can watch the news together."

Fang gave a weak smile. "That sounds better than doom scrolling in my apartment alone like I had planned."

Sherrie gave her friend a hug then the three of them headed to their respective apartments. Leroux went directly to the bedroom to change as Sherrie removed her bathing suit then lay on the bed. "I wonder if I'll get called up."

He shrugged as he eyeballed her naked body. She snapped the bikini top at him.

"Don't get any ideas, mister, you're on the clock."

He frowned. "You have no idea how hard you are to live with."

She eyeballed his crotch. "Oh, really?"

He turned his back to her. "Don't you be getting any ideas." He checked himself in the mirror as she rolled off the bed and joined him. She adjusted his tie and gave him a gentle kiss.

"You go save the world while Fang and I save a bottle of white wine from any further suffering in the fridge."

He eyed her. "You're going to be shit-faced by the time I get home, aren't you?"

"Yes, I am, and I give you prior consent to do with me what you will."

He grinned and his heart raced. He held up his phone. "Repeat that so I can record it."

She smacked his ass. "Get the hell out of here before the Chief sends a team to collect you."

33

He gave her a hug then headed for the door, wagging a finger over his shoulder. "Don't have too much fun tonight. No matter how sexy the rag doll looks, it's never any fun."

Acton/Palmer Residence

St. Paul, Maryland

"So, what do you think? Spain or India?"

Mai Trinh exchanged an excited glance with her boyfriend, Tommy Granger, and they both answered in unison. "India!"

James Acton chuckled. "I had a funny feeling you'd say that."

Mai shrugged. "It's no contest. We've been to Spain before, and we're not really going there to see anything, we're going there to relax. And while I don't mind that, I'd prefer to experience something, and India has always fascinated me."

"Me too," agreed Tommy. "So, what's this place this senator wants to go to called again?"

"It has several names, Skeleton Lake, Mystery Lake, Lake of Bones."

Tommy put an arm around Mai. "Sounds creepy. What's its story?"

"About eighty years ago, they discovered bones in a mountain lake. Over the decades, they've counted over three-hundred sets of remains, some still with flesh."

Mai's eyebrows shot up. "So they were killed recently?"

Acton shook his head. "No. The skeletons have been dated between two hundred and twelve-hundred years old, so it wasn't just a single event that killed these people. They died over a millennium, which is, of course, part of the mystery. Why did so many people die at this lake that's in the middle of nowhere?"

"But there's a bigger mystery," continued Laura Palmer. "While many of the bones belong to the people of that area, many of them were from regions far from India, including Europe. How Europeans ended up thousands of kilometers away from their homes to wind up in a lake in India has never been explained."

"So, we're going to go there and solve it?" asked Tommy, his eagerness clear.

Acton laughed. "While I admire your faith in our abilities, we're merely going there as sightseers. We'll get a tour of the area, I'll answer any questions the senator may have, then we'll leave. My guess is we'll be on the ground no more than a couple of hours. Then with my official duties over, we can take a tour of India."

"I want to see the Taj Mahal." Mai clasped her hands together, pumping them in front of her chest. "Every time I see a picture of that place, I just have this overwhelming urge to go there."

"Top of our list," agreed Acton. "But there are a lot of other incredible things to see there. India has a long history of an advanced civilization. We could spend months there and barely scratch the surface, but we'll have to squeeze everything into two weeks."

Tommy grunted. "I doubt we'll last two weeks."

Acton regarded the young man who had become part of their family by dating Mai, the young woman who had become like a daughter to them after helping save their lives and being forced into exile because of it. "What do you mean?"

"Well, Hugh's going to be with us, right?"

"Yes."

"I guarantee you, from the moment he steps off the plane, he's going to be bitching about the heat. Are you going to be able to stand two weeks of that?"

Acton roared with laughter. "I hadn't thought of that, but you're right. We better make sure every vehicle we're in has air conditioning or we'll never hear the end of it." His phone beeped and he picked it up, opening the message. "It's the senator's office. All of us have been cleared to attend."

"Even me?" asked Mai, a hint of doubt in her voice.

"Even you, my dear."

She hopped up and down in her chair with glee. "Before I met you, the world was only a place I read about. And even then, because of the Communist government, I was never sure if what I was reading was true. But now, thanks to you, I get to see the world."

Laura reached out and took the young woman's hand, squeezing it. "And thanks to you, we get to experience the joys of seeing these things again for the first time through your eyes."

Acton held up a hand. "Okay, everybody stop, otherwise we're just going to start crying. And I have to call Hugh and tell him not to pack for the beach."

Laura laughed, jabbing a finger at his phone. "You are putting that on speaker. I have to hear this."

Acton flashed some teeth as he dialed. He put the phone on speaker and set it on the table. Everyone leaned in as it was answered by their old Interpol friend, Hugh Reading.

"Jim, old boy, to what do I owe the pleasure?"

"Oh, I was just checking to see if you're still alive. You're getting up there, you know."

Reading's growl erupted from the phone. "If we were on FaceTime, you'd see what finger I was holding up."

Everyone laughed. "Hi, Hugh. How are you?" asked Laura.

"Wishing you had chosen a better husband."

"Yes, his sense of humor does leave something to be desired."

"So, why are you calling? You do realize what time it is here, don't you? I need my beauty sleep if I'm going to impress the ladies on the beach."

Acton snickered. "So, you've been working on your beach bod?"

"Bah. At my age, any woman's going to have to accept that any six-pack I might have had in my youth has long since retired, and gravity has conquered my chest. If anything's going to attract a woman, it's going to be my sparkling personality."

Acton winked at Laura. "It's going to be a lonely trip then, isn't it?"

"There are two fingers held up now. So, why *are* you calling?"

"Change of plans."

Reading groaned. "Please tell me you're not messing with my peaceful beach vacation. You do realize that the last time I managed to get away to Spain, you two screwed it up with that Templar business?"

"That wasn't exactly our fault."

"Oh, it never is. So, what have you gotten yourselves into now?"

"Don't worry, Hugh," said Laura. "It's nothing like that. Apparently, my husband's skills are needed by his government."

"This doesn't sound good."

She giggled. "A senator is going to India for some ceremony, and once his official duties are done, wants to see an archaeological site. We've all been invited to accompany him to the event, after which James will conduct a tour of the site. After that, we're free to do what we want. Our plan now is to tour India instead of lying on a beach."

A heavy sigh erupted from the other end. "India? Do you realize how far down the list of places I'd like to see that is?"

Acton leaned closer to the phone. "Think of the history that we'll get to see. The Taj Mahal, the Ganges, the—"

"The heat, the humidity, the smell of one-point-four-billion people all crammed into Scotland."

Laura shook her head. "India is a little bigger than Scotland."

"Yeah, a little."

"I promise you we'll have air conditioning everywhere possible."

"Unless you can strap one to my sagging ass, I have a feeling I'm going to be sweating my bollocks off for the entire two weeks."

Acton grinned at the others. "Well, with enough hiking and sweating, you might drop a cup size and discover one or two cans of your lost six-pack."

Reading growled. "Fine. I'll come with you. I've already booked the vacation time and my boss has insisted she absolutely doesn't want to see my face until next month. Besides, I know you two. You're going to get into some sort of trouble and you're going to need me to save your asses."

"That's the spirit. So, our initial plans haven't changed. We'll see you in London in two days, then head to India to meet up with the senator."

"Very well, but next time you plan a vacation, don't invite me until you're actually there. I can't take this kind of disappointment much more at this age."

Acton laughed and picked up his phone. "We'll see you in two days, buddy. Just try not to die before that."

"There are so many fingers pointing across the Atlantic right now."

Acton roared and ended the call then grinned at Laura. "Well, that went better than I expected."

Laura cocked an ear. "I think I can hear him swearing from here."

Mai snorted. "He reminds me of my grandfather. Always complaining but with a heart of gold."

Acton leaned back. "Well, if you want to keep experiencing that heart of gold, you better never let him hear you call him grandfather."

Outside Esztergom, Kingdom of Hungary
AD 1252

The meal had been delicious, in fact, one of the best Oldamur had ever had. That wasn't to say his wife wasn't a fantastic cook, it was simply that the ingredients available to her were the same he had grown up with and had eaten every day of his life. Tonight, he had indulged in things he had never even heard of, and while not all of it was to his liking, he had sampled everything. His wife had thoroughly enjoyed the experience as well, and now huddled with the women discussing what they had just eaten, one that spoke their language translating. The children had been pickier, of course, as children tended to be, and were now playing with the half-dozen others in the group, delighted to have new playmates, if only for an evening or two.

Pierre sat across from him, the fire between them crackling pleasantly, casting a gentle glow over the men that encircled it. "You asked who we were."

Oldamur's heart raced. Was he finally about to get the answers he so desperately craved? The meal's conversation had been pleasant, though nothing had been revealed about these people. Pierre was more interested in planning the work that needed to be done, and once settled, most of the conversations surrounded what they were eating and where it came from. He wasn't certain if these people were from the lands where these dishes originated, though he suspected so, and despite the lack of details, he had enjoyed himself. "Anything you would care to share would be very much appreciated, though I, of course, don't want to pry."

Pierre laughed. "We have nothing to hide, so ask your questions."

"You said you were pilgrims. Where are you going?"

"To a land far to the east where we can live in peace."

"Is there a war where you come from?"

Pierre shrugged. "For some of us, yes. For others, no. But peace isn't defined by a lack of war, is it? For example, here there is no war, but are you at peace?"

Oldamur looked about his farm. "I suppose. My wife and children and I are healthy. We can feed ourselves. What more can a man want?"

"Indeed. Many of those who are with me asked the same question as you did when we first met."

"Yet they're with you now."

"Indeed. And why do you think that is?"

Oldamur threw up his hands, shaking his head. "I have no idea. If they are as content as I am, I would see no reason to undertake a journey that sounds very distant."

"Oh, it is distant. It will probably take us years to reach there."

"Years?"

"Yes. I've made the trip myself three times in my life."

"Three times! Why would you do such a thing?"

"To share the paradise I have found with the worthy who so desperately need it." Pierre leaned forward. "May I ask you something very simple, very basic?"

"Of course."

"Do you feel oppressed?"

Oldamur thought for a moment. "I don't think so."

"Does your God not demand you follow rules that sometimes seem unreasonable?"

Oldamur shrugged. "If you're referring to the Ten Commandments, then I find them completely reasonable."

"Then let me rephrase. Do you find that those who administer to you, your priests, do you find them to be reasonable men?"

Oldamur thought of his meeting with Father Tamas and tensed.

Pierre picked up on it. "There is something, isn't there?"

Oldamur glanced about to make certain none of his neighbors had joined them in the dark. He opened his mouth to speak but thought better of it. It wasn't wise to criticize the Church or those who represented it.

Pierre regarded him with sympathy. "You see, this is exactly of what I speak."

Oldamur eyed him. "What do you mean?"

"Something is clearly troubling you, yet you're too scared to even share what it is with strangers who will be gone before the week is out, who will never repeat what you told them to anyone that knows you. Who is it you fear? Your God, your Church, your priest?"

Oldamur grunted. "All of them, I suppose."

Pierre sighed, shaking his head. "So sad that something that is supposed to bring comfort and joy should be feared instead. I can understand fearing a priest as he is but a man, and I can understand fearing the Church for it is but a creation of man, but to fear your own God, who is supposed to love you and protect you then welcome you into Heaven as your reward for being a good person while in this realm? To fear Him is truly sad, don't you think?"

Oldamur shrugged. "It's always been this way."

"Has it? Who taught you to fear your own God?"

Another shrug. "Our priests, I suppose. My parents."

"And who taught them?"

"Their priests, I suppose."

"Exactly. Have you ever actually read the Bible?"

"I can't read."

"So, no. Well, I have, and if you were to read the New Testament that speaks of your Lord Jesus Christ, you would weep, for nothing in there would ever have you fearing those you worship. So, I can assure you, God will not be angry if you share that which troubles you so."

Oldamur sighed. What did it matter? What was the worst that could possibly happen for sharing his troubles? Nothing had ever been said about keeping this a secret. His family wasn't the first to face such a crisis, and it wouldn't be the last, though he had never heard of a fee so high that it would leave a family destitute for the rest of their lives. He again sighed heavily. "I assume you've heard of indulgences?"

Pierre leaned back. "Ah, now I see. I am, of course, aware of them. It was why I left France so many years ago."

Oldamur paused. Could Pierre be a kindred spirit who would understand what it was that troubled him? Could he understand the unfairness of it all, the consequences? "What happened to you?"

Pierre leaned forward, poking the fire with a stick. "When I was a young man, my grandfather died and the local priest refused to perform the Last Rites, claiming my grandfather was a sinner who hadn't confessed, therefore couldn't be absolved of his sins. He offered us the option of paying for an indulgence—an invention of the Church, by the way. There is no mention of such a thing in the Bible. The sum was exorbitant, but my father was desperate to save his father's soul, so he paid it, ruining our household, for the amount was so large, most of our lands had to be sold.

"I learned later that my grandfather had a long-running dispute with the cardinal, and when my own father died from consumption a few years later, and he too was declared a sinner and the price to save his soul was more than what our estate was worth, I knew then that this had nothing to do with gaining anyone's entrance into Heaven, and everything to do with lining the pockets of those who had the power to issue indulgences. So, I walked away, but not before selling everything I could, then dividing it among those I employed. I then headed east to see if something better was out there beyond the reach of a corrupt church."

Oldamur extended a hand toward the others. "I assume you found it."

"I did, though it took me a long time. It was years before I found a place unspoiled by the Holy Roman Empire, where men believed in something different, where their spiritual guides weren't motivated by greed. I spent years among these people, learning their ways, and came to worship as they did. But in time, I began to feel guilty, for I was so happy, so at peace, while my countrymen and fellow Christians toiled in fear. So, I decided to return and save those whose lives had been destroyed by the corruption. This is my third trip. I have saved many families over the years from the fate their local priest would condemn them to, from a system that encouraged it so Rome could fund its empire. Have you seen the Vatican? Have you seen the churches being built throughout Europe? They all cost money, money that comes from people like you, desperate to save the souls of their loved ones." Pierre's voice became gentle. "Whose soul have they demanded payment for?"

Oldamur's eyes burned and his chin dropped to his chest. "My mother."

"And how much have they demanded to save her soul?"

"More than this farm is worth."

"And will you pay it?"

Oldamur's voice cracked. "I have no choice. It's my mother. While what you say may be true, that this is a corruption of the Church, I can't take that risk. I can't think of my poor, sweet mother damned for eternity because I've refused to pay."

"And how will you pay?"

Oldamur dried his eyes with the back of his hands. "All I can think to do is give them the farm."

"And then where will you go? How will you feed your wife and children?"

"I have no idea. I just found out yesterday, and I haven't had time to think."

"There is an alternative."

Oldamur looked up at Pierre. "And what's that?"

"Come with us."

Director Morrison's Office, CIA Headquarters

Langley, Virginia

Present Day

After being announced by the receptionist, Chris Leroux stepped into Leif Morrison's office. "Hey, Chief, you wanted to see me?"

Morrison didn't look up from his computer, instead pointing at one of the chairs in front of his desk. Leroux sat and waited. There was a time when this was intimidating, but now he was accustomed to being consulted directly by Morrison. The man had recognized something in him and had pushed him into the supervisory position he now held.

Fortunately, he had excelled.

He loved his job. He loved his team, though he had contemplated quitting when pushed into the new role. Fortunately, with friends like Sherrie and Kane bolstering his confidence, he had stuck with it. He was now well-respected, so much so that the Chief had confided in him that he might be running the show one day. That, he couldn't see, but anything was possible. Personally, he'd be content just doing what he was doing for the rest of his career.

Morrison finally finished reading whatever it was on his screen and leaned back. "Tell me what you know about China and India."

The question was laughably broad, and it was clear Morrison was exhausted. "One doesn't fill you up and the other gives you the runs."

Morrison stared at him blankly then finally chuckled. "Okay, I deserved that. The China-India situation at the border. What's the latest from your team?"

Leroux shrugged. "I read the latest briefs on my way in. The Chinese have moved in an additional division and have assembled enough air power in the region to overwhelm anything India could possibly put up against them if they decide they want to invade."

"What's that famous gut of yours telling you?"

Leroux scratched his chin, choosing his words carefully, for what he said could affect people's lives, as he found the Chief often went to Washington with the advice he gave. "I think they want to make a statement, and they want to test us. They want Taiwan, but don't know how we'll respond if they decide to take it. India is the test case. If they invade northeastern India, which is strategically unimportant to America and its allies, the public likely wouldn't care, but it would give the Chinese an opportunity to demonstrate what their capabilities now are. If I were them, the moment that communications facility is opened, I would send my troops across the border, secure a significant enough chunk of Indian territory for people to notice, then hold it for a few weeks, repelling any counterattacks before strategically withdrawing back within my borders, just to prove I can do it and that there was nothing anybody could do about it. It would certainly send a message to any of their neighbors of what could happen to them if they pissed off Beijing, and send a signal to us that should we decide to interfere with their expansion plans, we can get more than a bloody nose."

"And this tests us how?"

"If they make it a significant enough operation, India will ask for help. If we don't provide it, China may interpret that as the green light for Taiwan. If we do respond, they might think twice."

Morrison's head slowly bobbed. "Interesting." He paused. "We've got Senator Joseph Simmons attending the opening of that communications center. Do you think he's safe?"

"Yes, assuming we've made his attendance public. The Chinese wouldn't dare intentionally kill a US senator. It would demand a major response from us. This is all a show. They're counting on facing only the Indian military, which they think they can easily defeat. That gives them the publicity they're looking for, and makes them look like a superpower. Kill an American senator while staging their propaganda photo-op, they risk facing us as well, putting their favorable news coverage at risk."

"Could they hit the facility beforehand, before it opens?"

"They could, but then they wouldn't get the optics they're looking for. The Chinese want to look as if their actions are defensive in nature. Remember, it doesn't matter if the lie is believable to us. All that matters is that the lie is believable to their people, and their people have been conditioned to believe what the government tells them. So, I have no doubt that when that facility opens, the Chinese will have footage of the

50

ceremony playing on their newscasts within minutes, with news anchors their population trust telling them how provocative it is and how it puts China at risk. If they take it out beforehand, they'll appear to be the aggressor. Remember, the United Nations is mostly made up of despots and dictators. They outnumber the truly democratic nations of the world. They'll probably be able to get a resolution passed condemning India for its actions, America for its involvement, and praising China for defending itself from unprovoked aggression, especially when China promises to withdraw."

Morrison sighed. "The United Nations is a joke. We need a United Democratic Nations. If your people aren't allowed to vote in free and fair elections, and choose who speaks on their behalf, then you shouldn't have any say in how the world is governed."

"You're preaching to the choir, sir. The UN is one of the most corrupt organizations in the world. But putting that aside, I believe when the senator leaves, that's when the facility will be hit." Leroux frowned. "Knowing Senator Simmons' track-record, I'm guessing even if we urged him not to attend, he would."

Morrison gave a curt nod. "Agreed, but frankly, I'd do the same."

"If he's going to attend, I recommend he immediately leave the area and head west. New Delhi or preferably Mumbai. If the Chinese invade, they're not going to hit major population centers because they'll lose any support they might have. They're going to keep things restricted to the immediate region."

Morrison pursed his lips. "You really think they're going to invade?"

"I wouldn't bet my life on it, but yes, sir, I do believe the odds favor them invading."

Morrison sighed. "There's something you should be aware of."

"What's that?"

"Senator Simmons is an archaeology buff, and he intends to visit a site in the area, and by in the area I mean probably see the smoke from the communications center if it's taken out."

"That might not be wise."

"Agreed. Which is why I stacked the deck slightly in our favor, since I was aware that not only would he refuse to change his travel plans despite anything we might say to him, he also always invites a subject matter expert on these side trips. Someone from his state."

Leroux thought for a moment. "He's Maryland, isn't he?"

"Yes."

Leroux's eyes shot wide. "Are you telling me—"

Morrison cut him off. "Yes. I recommended he bring Professor Acton along."

Leroux closed his eyes. "So, this time *we're* intentionally putting them in danger?"

"Someone was going to be put in danger regardless. At least the professors have the ability to take care of themselves."

"Against the entire Chinese Army?"

Morrison chuckled. "I wouldn't put it past them, but no. I'm thinking more about level-headedness. When the shit hits the fan, they don't panic. They're more likely to be able to save themselves than some common civilian off the street. Just because we know them doesn't mean their lives are any more valuable than any other American citizen."

Leroux frowned. "I suppose morally that's true, but these people are friends to this agency and to our Special Forces, especially with what they did for them a couple of weeks ago."

Morrison held up a hand. "You're right, which is why I've had Bravo Team assigned to the region. Their mission is to extract our delegation should it become necessary."

Leroux eyed Morrison. "You mean Delta's going to be on scene?"

"No, the Indians would never agree to that. However, should things go south, I have unofficial assurances that they'll be allowed in unchallenged."

Leroux grunted. "I wonder if they said that because they feel the Chinese aren't a threat, or if they feel they are, and if they can get an American soldier killed because of it, it's more likely to get us involved."

Morrison shifted in his chair, appearing uncomfortable.

Leroux regarded him. "We're getting involved, aren't we?"

Morrison stared at him for a moment, as if debating whether to say something. "This is repeated to no one, and I mean *no* one. Girlfriends, best friends, I don't care, you're not to speak of it until I officially inform you of it."

Leroux tensed. "Of course, sir."

Morrison leaned forward and lowered his voice, despite there being no chance of anyone hearing him outside of this room. "The president has already sent Carrier Strike Group Five into the area, which of course isn't exactly a secret—you can't move a carrier group with nobody noticing—but he's put our forces in the region on standby. You might be happy to know that the White House and its Pentagon advisors agree with you, that China is likely to invade, and if they succeed with no reaction from us, it will not only send the message the Chinese want to the region and to the world, but it will embolden them further, not to mention the Russians. America has sat by for so long doing nothing to challenge countries like China and Russia, that the president fears, as do his advisors, that should the Chinese be allowed to invade India, Taiwan will be next, and that could lead to all-out war."

Leroux's heart raced. "So, what you're saying is that if the Chinese invade, we're intervening?"

"Unless opinions change at the White House, the orders will be to engage anything in the air that crosses the Indian border. Rules of Engagement will limit our forces from crossing the Chinese border or firing into it, or firing on troops on the ground. The orders are to establish air superiority and maintain it, so that Indian ground forces have a chance to engage the Chinese forces."

"But with so many troops, do the Indians have any hope of engaging them successfully?"

"Don't forget the Indians have an air force as well. If they can operate unencumbered, they'll be able to decimate Chinese ground forces. If Chinese casualties are heavy, they just might rethink this. Remember the region we're talking about here. This isn't wide open spaces like Europe in World War Two. This is trying to fit 200,000 troops across a limited number of bridges and roads. The moment the Chinese cross the border, the president will issue his warning for them to immediately pull back as our fighters are scrambled, and if the Chinese don't halt their advance, they will be engaged."

Leroux whistled through his teeth. "*This* could lead to all-out war. Forget Taiwan."

"Possibly, though by limiting our actions to occur only in Indian airspace, and by providing them with plenty of warning, we're hoping to minimize the chances of the conflict escalating."

Leroux exhaled heavily. "Too often these things have a way of getting out of control. An itchy trigger finger on one of those pilots currently buzzing Taiwan could change this into an all-out shooting war across the entire Pacific and Indian subcontinent."

"Let's hope you're wrong and that in the end, cooler heads prevail. There's still a chance the Chinese are just making a bunch of noise and have no intention of crossing the border."

Leroux grunted. "That might have been a possibility yesterday, but you just sent the world's two biggest magnets for trouble into the area. With the professors there, this is definitely turning into a Charlie-Foxtrot."

Outside Esztergom, Kingdom of Hungary

AD 1252

It had been a long, difficult conversation in bed with his wife after Pierre had made the offer to join his pilgrimage. Even Oldamur wasn't convinced it was the wisest of moves, but the conversation had to be held. This was the first opportunity he had had to tell his wife of the fee demanded by Father Tamas, the topic simply too difficult to broach the previous night. She had sobbed at the amount, and even more so when she realized the only way to pay it was to give up everything they owned. His heart was warmed, however, at the words she spoke after she pushed past the self-pity.

"We could live with my brother and his family. They would take us in, I'm sure of it, and they have enough room for us to build ourselves a home and work his farm with him until we figure out a way to take care of ourselves."

His chest ached at how much he loved this woman, of how selfless she truly was. "So, you would be willing to give up everything to save my mother?"

"Of course I would! If there is any chance to save her soul, then we must do it. There's no question."

He hugged her hard and they both sobbed. When he finally regained control, he gently pushed her away. "There is an alternative to living with your brother that we should discuss."

She sniffed and wiped her nose on a handkerchief gripped in her hand. "And what's that?"

"Pierre has invited us to join his group."

She gasped. "On their pilgrimage?"

"Yes."

"But from what I can gather from the women, it could be years of travel."

"Yes, it could be. It would be difficult. We would suffer greatly, I'm certain. But when it was over, we would live in peace in what Pierre said could only be described as a paradise."

"Do you believe him?"

"I do." He sighed. "If we're agreed that we're going to give the Church everything to save my mother's soul, then the coming years, perhaps even the rest of our lives, will be difficult. It's something I doubt we'll ever recover from. But if we join the others, within a few years we could be living in a new land, free from those who would take everything from us because they claimed my mother was a heretic. You saw these people. You met them, you ate with them, you spoke with them. Do they seem like good people?"

She nodded fervently. "Absolutely."

"And I feel the same. They're people just like us, escaping the tyranny of the Church to lead better lives in a community where we can worship the way we want, in peace with like-minded people."

"It sounds wonderful."

"It will be, and our lives will be our own again. My mother will have been saved, and our children will have a future. And should they decide to return, they'll be free to do so. From what Pierre describes, there are no rules, only that we live in peace with each other and respect each other."

She glanced about their bedroom. "I can't imagine leaving this all behind."

Oldamur's chest collapsed. "Soon, all of this belongs to the Church regardless, whether we stay or not."

His wife wiped away the tears that flowed once again. "It's so unfair."

He held her in his arms, gently stroking her back. "Yes, it is, but you know there's no way to fight the Church, and there's no way we can change Father Tamas' mind."

"Could we go over his head, perhaps speak to the bishop?"

"How would we ever get a meeting? And the likelihood of him overruling and therefore undermining our new priest is slim. All we might do is delay the inevitable and make our lives here even more difficult. I believe with Pierre, we have a once-in-a-lifetime opportunity. Everybody arrives with nothing but what they can carry. Our skills will be assessed and we'll be put to work. I think he called it a commune. The entire group owns everything and works collectively so no one goes hungry. Everyone has a roof over their head, and everyone protects each other."

"It sounds like paradise."

"From what he described, it certainly does." He smiled at her. "And there are no winters."

She gasped. "No winters? How is that even possible?"

He shrugged. "I don't know, but he assures me where they live, we'll never see another snowflake unless it's atop a mountain."

She rested her head on his chest. "To never be cold again, to never be hungry because of a bad harvest..." She twisted in his arms and stared at him. "I say we join them."

He smiled down at her. "Are you sure? It will be difficult."

"And life here isn't? Let's give the Church the farm, save your mother's soul, and never look back."

"It will mean leaving our friends and family behind."

"I know, but the moment we give up the farm, we'll become a burden to all of them, and burden can lead to resentment. If Pierre is right and life is indeed as wonderful as he describes, then we can send word and have them come join us if they so wish."

Oldamur drew a deep breath then exhaled loudly, squeezing her tight. "Then it is settled. We will join Pierre in his paradise and leave our troubles behind."

Indira Gandhi International Airport

New Delhi, India

Present Day

Acton stepped onto the tarmac, the heat oppressive, waves dancing before his eyes as it radiated off the pavement. This was the only time where taking a commercial flight beat private—there was no air-conditioned jetway attached to the door of the plane leading them inside the terminal. Instead, they had to walk across this outdoor baking sheet before the charter terminal would provide them with relief.

He helped Laura down then Mai. Tommy followed then Reading appeared in the doorway. "Bloody hell. This is bollocks."

Acton eyed him. "We were going to lie on a beach in Spain. Not exactly an air-conditioned vacation."

Reading stepped down, positioning his sunglasses. "No comparison. When I'm lying on a beach underneath my umbrella, I can be the dirty old man everybody thinks I am and enjoy the sights. Here?" He waved a hand at their surroundings. "What have I got to look at?"

Laura eyed him. "And just what would those sights on the beach have been?"

Reading cleared his throat as his cheeks flushed. "The waves and the sand."

Laura pointed at her breasts. "You sure you're not talking about these things?"

Reading's jaw dropped as his head spun away, holding out a hand to block his line of sight. "I most certainly do not stare at, you know, your chestal region."

"I would hope not. Beaches are filled with beautiful young women with bodies a hell of a lot better than mine."

Acton leaped to his wife's body's defense from the unwarranted attack by its owner. "I'll have you know there are women half your age that would kill to have your body."

Laura gave him the stink eye. "Just how old do you think I am?"

Acton scrambled to dig himself out of the inadvertent hole he had dug as they walked toward the terminal. He shook his head and held both hands up in surrender. "I'm staying out of this, but I suggest we change the subject before you give poor Hugh a coronary."

"Yes, please," agreed Reading, who sighed in ecstasy as they stepped through the door and into the air-conditioned building.

A young man in a business suit strode up to them, a broad practiced smile on his face. "Professor Acton?"

Acton bowed his head slightly. "Yes."

"I'm Kamal Khatri from the Ministry of Culture. I'm here to expedite your clearance through customs, then you and your party will be handed over to a representative from the American embassy."

Acton shook the man's hand. "Thank you very much. It's appreciated." His eyes swept the small terminal, noting more security than normally expected. "Is something going on?"

Khatri turned his head to see what Acton was looking at. "Just a precaution. As I'm sure you're aware, China is being its usual belligerent self. We've added more security to public spaces simply to reassure the citizenry that they're safe."

"And are we?" asked Reading, his commanding voice startling the young man.

"Oh, I can assure you, you're perfectly safe here."

"And where we're going?"

The young man shrugged. "I'm sorry, sir. I'm not privy to that information." He spun on his heel, beckoning them to follow as he headed toward the customs set up, clearly in a rush.

Acton glanced at Reading, lowering his voice slightly. "Do you get the impression he's holding back on us?"

Reading grunted. "Absolutely. Hopefully, our embassy rep will be more forthcoming."

They quickly cleared security and Khatri walked them up to a man whose back was facing them, his tan cargo shorts and untucked white shirt suggesting a far more casual dress code than where the young Indian worked.

"Mr. White?"

The man turned with a broad smile and quickly reached out and grabbed Acton's hand, pumping it before Acton could reveal his surprise. "Professor Acton, it's a pleasure to meet you. Jack White, here from the American Embassy. Now, I know we've never met before, but I feel like I know you after reading your file. I can see why the senator chose you and your lovely wife to play tour guide for him."

It took a moment for Acton to recover from the shock of seeing Jack—just Jack, as the man liked to call himself—a CIA operative that had saved their asses in Mongolia. "Pleasure to meet you, Mr. White, was it?"

"Yes, but just call me Jack."

Acton "introduced" the others, all as stunned as he was, though everyone played the game.

Jack extended a hand to Khatri. "Thank you so much for getting them through customs so quickly."

"My pleasure, Mr. White." Khatri bowed to Acton and the others, then headed out of the terminal with nothing else said, the man's pleasantness no doubt covering up the fact he didn't appreciate the menial task he'd been handed by his superiors.

Jack held out a hand. "I have a vehicle waiting outside for you."

"Air-conditioned, I hope," muttered Reading.

"Absolutely. You know, a buddy of mine told me you can apparently buy a wearable air conditioner now. I've offered him a month's pay to get me one. I'll have that thing strapped to my boys so fast, you'll think it had always been there."

Reading laughed and jabbed a finger at Jack. "That's what I said two days ago, though I strapped it somewhere more dignified!"

"Where?"

"My ass."

"Great minds think alike."

"And fools seldom differ," piped in Tommy with a grin.

Both Jack and Reading spun their heads quickly at the young man, giving him the stink eye. Tommy shrunk behind Mai before the two roared with laughter. "Just messin' with ya kid," said Jack as he indicated a large Ford Expedition ahead. He climbed behind the wheel and Acton opened the passenger side door, motioning at Reading to get inside.

"You take the front seat unless you want to snuggle with my wife whose tatas you apparently stare at on the beach."

Reading's eyes shot wide, his cheeks a healthy crimson. He finally shook a fist at Acton. "Respect your elders."

Acton burst out laughing and slapped the man on the back. "Get inside. You can play with the air conditioning dials instead of—"

"James!" admonished Laura.

Acton gave her a sheepish look. "Did I cross the line?"

Jack roared. "Dude, you pole-vaulted over the line."

Laura gave her husband the eye. "If you plan on doing any dialing on this trip, leave poor Hugh alone."

"Thank you," said Reading, giving Acton the finger before climbing in and slamming the door shut. The rest piled in and Jack started the engine, Reading aiming every nozzle he could at every part of his body they could reach. He sighed. "Now that's better."

Jack chuckled as he pulled away from the curb. "I forgot how much fun it was working with you people. You're all nuts."

Acton leaned forward between the seats. "And you're not?"

"Oh, I'm definitely nuts. That's why I like working with you."

Now that they were alone, Acton asked the question they were all dying to know the answer to. "So, why are you here?"

"Some chief in North America thought you could use some help here in India."

"Chief?" asked Tommy.

"Not that kind of chief."

Acton leaned back. "Uh-huh. Help, my ass. What's really going on? What aren't you telling us?"

"My mission, which I was given no choice but to accept, is to exfil your asses should something go wrong."

Laura exchanged a glance with Acton, taking his hand. "Just what could go wrong?"

"You have been watching the news, haven't you? There's a little situation brewing between India and China."

Reading twisted in his seat to face Jack. "I thought that was just posturing. Nothing to be taken seriously."

"Yes, that's what most of those expert talking heads on your twenty-four-hour news channels are telling you, but our people think it could go beyond that."

"Do they really think so?" asked Laura. "Do they really think there could be war?"

"They think there's a distinct possibility. They're not saying absolutely, and the going theory is that if they do invade, they won't do so until the senator has left the communications center."

Acton tensed. "That doesn't sound good."

"No, it doesn't. Which is why I've convinced the senator's team to change your itinerary."

"Oh?"

"Instead of attending the ceremony then going to the archaeological site, you'll instead be going to the site first and then to the ceremony. As soon as the ceremony is over, you'll be taken out of the area along with the senator. Should the Chinese decide to do anything, you'll be safely out of the conflict zone."

Laura's hand tightened its grip. "Just how far from the border are we?"

"Skeleton Lake is about thirty miles from the border. Not very far at all."

"And this communications facility?"

"It's on the other side of the mountain, not very far as the crow flies. There's a road that cuts through the area. You can actually drive from the site to the communications facility. We're going to fly you to the site by helicopter to do your tour, then you'll be taken by car to the communications center in time for the ceremony. The ceremony is merely a formality—a couple of hours at most. Once the formalities are done, we get you on your chopper and you head to safety. If everyone behaves and the Chinese stick to protesting and stay on their side of the border, this will be much ado about nothing."

"Fingers crossed," said Tommy from the back row.

Jack flashed a grin in the rearview mirror. "Don't worry. It sounds a lot scarier than it is. If the powers that be truly thought it was dangerous, they might still send you in, but they'd never send the senator."

Acton grunted. "I suppose that's true. So, are you our babysitter?"

"No, I'll be doing my hair and reorganizing my sock drawer. I'm just dropping you off at your hotel, then you probably won't see me again." He became serious. "But if you do see me, be prepared to do whatever I say, no questions asked."

Acton frowned. "Then don't take this the wrong way, but I hope we don't see you again."

USS Barry, Carrier Strike Group 5
Arabian Sea

"Is it weird that I'm craving Indian food?"

Command Sergeant Major Burt "Big Dog" Dawson glanced up from his tablet at Sergeant Carl "Niner" Sung, his own stomach giving a sympathy rumble.

"Of course it's weird," boomed Sergeant Leon "Atlas" James, his impossibly deep voice rumbling through the room they were sequestered in while awaiting what had the potential to become World War III. "Every time we go somewhere, you crave the local cuisine."

Niner gave Atlas a look. "I don't recall once craving borscht on our last mission."

"Borscht? Nobody in their right mind has ever craved borscht," commented Sergeant Eugene "Jagger" Thomas, his monster lips protruding from his scrunched-up face.

Sergeant Will "Spock" Lightman cocked an eyebrow. "This from the man I saw eating crickets last month when we were in Thailand. I'd eat borscht all day every day if it meant not eating bugs."

Jagger shrugged. "You're one to talk. I've seen you shoving snails down your throat whenever Joanne would make them. You couldn't—" He stopped himself, his face sagging at his faux pas. He leaned toward the now silent Spock. "I'm sorry, brother, I shouldn't have mentioned her."

Spock waved off the apology. "No, avoiding mentioning her doesn't honor her memory. It's just that it's still too raw not to react." He drew a deep breath. "And her schnecken was the best."

Niner's eyes narrowed. "Schnecken? I thought snails were called escargot."

"The French call them escargot, the Germans call them schnecken. Her mother was born in Germany and taught her all the recipes from back home."

Dawson leaned back and smiled at the memories of their last dinner party. They were all Non-Commissioned Officers, NCOs, members of 1st Special Forces Operational Detachment—Delta, known to the public as the Delta Force. And dinner parties were rare. He and the guys were accustomed to beer and pizza or a barbecue, but every once in a while the women in their lives arranged something civilized that didn't end in belching contests. After a mission that had taken them to Germany, Joanne had been inspired and hosted a dinner party with nothing but German food. It was a heavy meal, though so good. Pork schnitzel with spaetzle couldn't be beaten if prepared by someone who knew what they were doing. And Joanne certainly knew what she was doing.

Had known.

Dawson reached over and gave Spock's shoulder a squeeze. "We all miss her, brother, especially her cooking."

Spock leaned forward, hanging his head between his knees. His shoulders shook and a single sob escaped. Everyone in the room rose, wanting to comfort their grieving friend, but Spock held up a hand then sniffed deeply before sitting upright. "Sorry about that. Like I said, it's still raw."

Jagger sat and his shoulders slumped. "I'm sorry, brother. I shouldn't have said anything."

Spock shook his head. "No, like I said, she should be honored. She was my wife, the mother of my daughter, and she was my best friend. I never want to forget any of that."

Dawson's head bobbed slowly in agreement. "The Unit is our family, this team is a family, and family goes beyond those of us in this room. It includes Joanne and your daughter, it also includes Vanessa, Angela, Maggie. She was a good friend to us all, she was a great wife, a great mother."

"A great cook," added Jagger.

Atlas leaned back. "And a kick-ass softball player. That girl could pitch. I could never hit anything off her."

Niner eyed the impossibly muscled Atlas. "You can't hit anything off anyone with those brontosaurus drumsticks you call arms."

"I hit anything you throw."

"That's because I love you and go easy on you so that you don't embarrass yourself."

"Bullshit, you just throw like a pansy."

"Only to you, my dear, only to you."

Spock wiped his eyes dry with a knuckle. "There's a reason you two are almost always on the same team. It's because neither of you can be trusted to play your best against the other."

Atlas leaned back, puzzled. "Wait a minute. You mean to tell me when you guys are picking teams, you're skipping over me if the other guy's got Niner?"

"And vice versa."

"Well, I'll be a son of a bitch. How long have you guys been doing that?"

Spock shrugged. "Ever since the love affair began."

Niner grinned and Atlas flipped birds at everyone, laughter erupting.

Dawson's secure phone vibrated with an update from Control, upgrading their status. He wagged the phone in the air. "Okay, ladies, listen up. Our mission is to exfil a group of American and British nationals from the China-India border should things go south with the opening of India's new communications facility. What you haven't been told yet is who those nationals are." He held up his phone to make a show of it, though he didn't need it—these names were ingrained in his mind. "Professor—"

As soon as the word was out of his mouth, the entire room groaned in exaggerated exasperation. Everyone to a man would lay down their lives for the professors.

"—James Acton, Professor Laura Palmer, Interpol Agent Hugh Reading, Thomas Granger, and Mai Trinh."

Niner's eyes narrowed. "I thought you said American and British? Isn't Mai Vietnamese?"

"She got her citizenship recently."

Niner smiled broadly, as did the others. Mai had risked her life to save theirs and had paid a hefty price—exiled from her country, never to see her family again.

"Good for her," said Atlas. "She's a good kid."

"Yes, good for her, but why, pray tell, are they in India, near the border where 200,000 Chinese regulars have gathered?" asked Jagger.

"Senator Simmons is an archaeology buff and wants to visit a site nearby after the ceremony. He invited Professor Acton to be his guide, and the others came along as guests. My briefing indicates they were all going on vacation together, and this interrupted their plans." Dawson tapped his phone. "It says here that their itinerary has changed. They're going to the archaeological site first, attending the opening ceremony, then leaving immediately afterward. Assuming the Chinese behave themselves, we'll stand down. If they don't, and the professors' existing itinerary is interrupted, we go in."

Sergeant Zack "Wings" Hauser raised a finger. "Just to clarify, are we only here for the five people on that list, or are we also here for the senator and his people?"

"Both, however the senator and his people have their own security team. We're to provide assistance should it be needed."

Atlas squinted as he peered at Dawson. "Wait a minute here. Why was the Doc chosen to be the guide? There have to be thousands of archaeologists back home that could have fit the bill. Why was he chosen?"

Dawson tilted his head for a moment. "That's the $64,000 question, isn't it? According to the colonel, *we* were specifically requested two days ago."

"Requested by whom?"

"Langley."

Niner's eyebrows shot up. "Wait a minute, are you suggesting that Langley chose the Doc to head into the middle of what might be one hell of a firefight?"

"It's a possibility. I read the briefing notes on the senator. Apparently, he does these side trips all the time, and always brings someone from his home state along with him as an advisor."

Atlas' mouth opened slightly. "Ah, this senator wouldn't happen to be from the great state of Maryland, would he?"

"He would."

"So, he was taking someone regardless."

Niner eyed his friend. "So what? Someone at Langley thought it would be best to put in some professors with combat experience?"

Atlas shrugged. "Could be."

Niner shook his head. "Man, that's cold. After everything they've done for us and their country."

"I get the distinct impression that the current situation isn't what was planned for," said Dawson.

"Why's that?" asked Wings.

"The briefing package I received initially only listed the professors. The updated package adds the other three, plus a note that all five funded their own trip with the senator's approval. If Langley did indeed recommend the professors for the trip, I don't think they intended for them to be accompanied by two kids in their mid-twenties and an aging British detective nearing retirement."

"Then why not just call it off?"

"I asked the colonel that, and he said the senator is not willing to give in to the Chinese."

"Then he's not going to be happy about his itinerary being changed. If he's getting on a chopper and heading out of the country the moment they cut the ribbon, it sort of looks like he's running from them."

"Regardless, our status has been upgraded. Everyone do a bladder check, then we'll do another equipment check. If the shit hits the fan, we're leaving on a moment's notice, and all we'll have is what we take in with us." Dawson rose, and the others followed. "Let's hope the Chinese behave themselves and remain behind their border, despite what the latest news reports suggest. As much as I'd like to make a small payment toward what we owe the professors for what they did for us a few weeks ago, I'd rather leave that debt unpaid if it means we avoid a war."

One month from paradise

AD 1255

To say the journey had been difficult would be an understatement, and if Oldamur had known just how difficult, he might not have committed his family to the arduous pilgrimage. As they had moved through the countryside and made camp near villages and towns along the way, more had joined their flock over the years. They now numbered almost 100, and would have numbered almost 200 if they hadn't lost so many. At least half a dozen families had turned around, unwilling to continue forward, to push through the pain, the constant trudging. Others had died from accidents, others from disease, even a few from foul play, murdered by brigands who would occasionally assail the group, only to find they had nothing of value.

But Pierre assured them they were nearly there, not even a month's journey remaining, and the excitement was building. Everything was so different than what they were used to, but they had finally entered the lands where the language Pierre had been teaching them was spoken. It made their interactions with the locals that much easier, even if they bore little resemblance to the ragtag group. Now that they had turned south, the skin of the people was dark, far darker than any tan he had seen. Hair was darker and thicker, and the clothing was unlike any he could have imagined in his wildest dreams.

It was at once intimidating, but also exciting, for it was everything Pierre had described. Oldamur was doing well with things and found he didn't miss home. His parents were dead, his grandparents long dead, and he was content with the knowledge that his siblings were happy, and as the eldest, he had saved them the burden of paying for their mother's entrance into the Kingdom of Heaven. Tears had been shed by their family and friends during the days leading up to their departure, but proper goodbyes had been made.

Father Tamas had been shocked, though unable to contain his glee once the farm was signed over to the Church. The indulgence had been issued, and if Tamas was to be believed, Oldamur's mother had been led through the gates by St. Peter the moment the seal was applied. In what was once their home, their business and lives were finished.

Along the way, they had made friends among the families. Everyone was in the same situation. They had all left everything behind, everyone behind, and as more of them became proficient in the language of their new home, that pool of friends grew as lines of communication opened. His wife had made many friends as well, though he had caught her crying alone on occasion. With word they were almost there, however, she seemed in a brighter mood. The children appeared unaffected, making new friends quickly and easily. They had grown much during the journey and adapted well, mastering the new language with little effort, and were already contributing members to their tiny society.

Everything suggested they had made the right decision, though he would be happy when the constant walking was finished. When the roads were wide, lined by grasslands where the children could play, the journey wasn't too bad. However, the mountain passes through which they now headed had them too often facing narrow paths with sheer cliff faces where if one lost their footing, they would certainly die.

And there was no stopping—they had to continue walking until they came to an area where they could rest and set up camp. Yet despite all this, miraculously, Pierre always knew precisely how far the next place to rest was.

"There it is!" shouted Pierre from the head of their column, his arm outstretched. Oldamur pushed up on his toes to see the promised village ahead, a place where they would be welcome to set up camp for several days to recharge for the final push to their own slice of Heaven on Earth.

"I can't see, Father."

Oldamur lifted his daughter over his head, placing her on his shoulders. "Now, can you see?"

"Yes, I can! Is this really the last village we'll see before we reach our new home?"

"Apparently. The last part will be difficult, but the rewards will be great. We only have to be strong for a little while longer."

The column moved forward, excitement in the air with the knowledge that respite was soon at hand. There was some jostling ahead, then a scream tore through the exuberance.

A child.

He lifted his daughter off his shoulders and put her down, pressing his family against the cliff face to their left, as far from the edge as he could. A woman wailed, reverting to her native tongue, and even though he didn't understand a word of what she was saying, her meaning was clear. She was begging for help. A hush swept through the group stretched out along the narrow trail, and he gently weaved through those in front of him, unwilling to compound what might already be a tragedy.

He reached the wailing woman and found a group of people peering over the edge of the cliff. "What happened?"

"My daughter fell over the edge!"

No one was taking charge, perhaps because there was nothing to take charge of—the child was already dead. As if to make a liar of him, the little girl called out weakly for her mother, and more people pushed to the edge in an attempt to see her, the jostling threatening further tragedy.

"Everybody stop!" he commanded. The crowd froze and turned to him. "Somebody else is going to get pushed over the edge!" He pointed at the group closest to the village. "All of you keep heading to the village. If anyone has some rope, bring it now." Those ahead reluctantly continued on, and those around him wised up, carefully guiding those behind them past the scene. The crowd calmed, and with the risk of another going over the edge dealt with, Oldamur kneeled and stretched out on his stomach. He inched forward and peered over the edge. He spotted the child on an outcropping below.

"Help me!" she screamed in their new language, most of the children her age having forgotten their mother tongue.

He held out his hand. "Remain calm, child. We'll be coming to get you very soon. Are you hurt?"

She sniffed heavily then shook her head. "I don't think so."

"Can you wiggle your fingers and toes?"

She made a show of it and giggled. "Yes."

"You can move your arms and they don't hurt?"

She flailed them around a bit. "They're all right."

"Good. Now, carefully move closer to the edge of the rock so that you're away from the drop."

She shuffled back from the edge.

"Good. Now, just stay there. I'll be coming for you soon."

"I've got some rope here," said one of the men.

"Good, give me an end. I'll tie it around my waist, then you two lower me down."

The small rescue crew set to work and moments later, Oldamur was over the edge, his heart hammering. He had never done anything like this before. He had never considered himself a brave man, and he still didn't, though he had never considered himself a coward either. He was simply doing what needed to be done, what was necessary—what he prayed someone would do for his children should they be in danger.

He suddenly jerked down a body length and scraped against the rock, the razor-sharp stones slicing into his knee. "Slowly!" he shouted as he stared above him. His wife was on her belly, peering over the ledge at him, terror on her face, but he couldn't see the two men holding the rope.

"Sorry!" called one of them. "There's not enough room up here."

Oldamur glanced down below. He was still too far from the outcropping holding the little girl. The rope jerked again and this time he dropped half a body length. He stared up to shout again at them when a foot appeared, gravel tumbling toward him. He closed his eyes and pressed his chin to his chest as the small stones rained down on him.

"Look out!"

Someone cried out in terror. He opened his eyes and stared up to see one of the men tumbling over the edge. The rope let go and he dropped the remaining distance, slamming into the ledge beside the crying child. He heard a crack and roared in agony as his lower leg snapped. Yet there was no time to deal with it. He used his good foot to push back against the cliff face then grabbed the rope with both hands. The screaming man flew past him, falling quickly out of sight, then the rope jerked tight. Oldamur was yanked forward and slid toward the edge but managed to jam his foot against an upturned part of the rock. His entire body rose into the air with the exception of the one foothold before the momentum of the falling man halted abruptly. Oldamur fell back down onto the cold rock, the screams continuing below.

"Calm down!" he shouted. "I've got you, but you need to help me!"

The struggling on the rope settled as did the pleas to God. "Are-are you sure you've got me?"

"Yes, but you're going to need to climb up. I've got a broken leg. Just hurry up."

His body jerked with each tug on the rope, and as the man worked his way up, he would occasionally find a foothold or a handhold that eased the tension off the rope, allowing Oldamur to draw up some of the slack, speeding up the process. After too much effort, he was joined on the small outcropping by an eternally grateful man who hugged him. "Thank you! Thank you so much! I don't know how I'll ever repay you."

Oldamur returned a thumping hug. "There's no need to repay me, though I will hand responsibility for saving this little girl to you. My leg is broken."

The man leaned forward and examined Oldamur's leg. "That looks pretty bad."

"Is everyone all right?" someone shouted from above.

Oldamur tilted his head back. "I have a broken leg, but your friend is all right." He turned to his companion. "Rahim, isn't it?"

"Yes. I joined you a few months ago with my family."

"We're going to need more rope!" shouted the man from overhead. "Give us a few moments!"

"Husband, are you all right?"

He smiled at the sound of his wife. "I'm fine, though I broke my leg." Her gasp could be heard even from his precipitous position. "Don't worry, I'll be fine once they get me up there."

"Here they come now," she reported, the relief in her voice unmistakable.

"We've got more rope. Here it comes."

Rahim grabbed the loose end as it swung in front of them. "You go first."

Oldamur shook his head. "No, the girl goes."

"She's too young to go alone. She has to go up with one of us, and that means me. So, you're going first."

Oldamur sighed. The man was right. "Very well." He patted the rope still around his waist. "We'll leave this one in place so we can use it as a second line when I get to the top."

Rahim agreed and added the second rope around Oldamur's waist. He indicated the broken leg. "This is going to hurt."

Oldamur had a feeling that was an understatement. He had broken bones before, of course. Accidents happened on the farm, but never in his life had he been dragged up a cliff face with a fracture dangling below. Yet he had no choice—the sooner he was up, the sooner the little girl would be safe. He tugged twice on the rope. "I'm ready!"

"Here we go!" called a voice from above.

The slack was removed and the rope tugged on his waist. Rahim bravely rose beside him on the sliver of outcropping and helped him to his feet. As soon as the broken leg was in the air, Oldamur gasped in agony, then when it slammed into the cliff face, he cried out, and his world fell dark.

Pullman New Delhi Aerocity Hotel

New Delhi, India

Present Day

Jack had been true to his word. He had dropped them off at their hotel and they hadn't seen him since. Everyone was assembled in their suite, bags all lined up by the door. Whoever had changed the itinerary had certainly made things more inconvenient. The original plan had them flying by helicopter to the ceremony, already dressed for it. They would then change into their casual clothes for the journey to the archaeological site. If there were one thing Acton was most sure of, it was that changing into casual clothes was a hell of a lot easier than changing into formal, doubly so if done in some cramped bathroom at an Indian military facility likely never expecting civilians.

He gestured toward Laura's gown hanging on the back of the door. "You're not bringing that?"

She shook her head. "No. Mai and I discussed it, and we're both wearing pantsuits. That's classy enough for this type of gathering."

83

Acton groaned with mock disappointment. "But I was so looking forward to seeing you in it."

"You have no idea," muttered Tommy.

Everyone turned toward him and his cheeks flushed. "I meant Mai in hers!" he quickly stammered.

Acton chuckled. "Well, I guess you, me, and Hugh will have to impress everyone with our tuxedos."

"Tuxedos?" Reading glared at him. "Nobody said anything about a damn tuxedo. It's bad enough I have to wear a suit in this infernal heat."

"I thought we told you this was a black-tie affair?"

Reading wagged a finger. "No, you told me it was a formal affair. To me, that's suit and tie. That's not tuxedos."

Acton scratched his chin. "I wonder if it's too late to rent you one?"

Reading checked his watch. "Bloody hell, of course there's no time! We're leaving in ten minutes!"

Laura frowned. "They might not let you in. You might have to stay outside."

"Outside in the heat?"

Laura leaned over and patted his cheek. "Even in India, the mountains are cool. You'll be fine. If anything, you'll be dealing with rain or snow. Did you bring a jacket?"

"Did I bring a jacket? It's India. Of course I didn't bring a jacket."

Acton decided he better let his friend off the hook before he suffered a coronary. "I'm just shitting with you, buddy. Suit and tie is fine. That's all I'm wearing. You know how I feel about those monkey suits."

Reading tossed his head back and growled. "You are so infuriating sometimes."

Laura giggled and Reading directed his wrath toward her. "And you're not innocent in all of this, young lady. You played right along with him."

She shrugged. "A girl's gotta have her fun."

Tommy pointed at the television, tuned to the BBC World News, the muted footage now indicating breaking news. Acton reached for the remote and turned up the volume, but the headline had already quashed any frivolity in the room.

Chinese fighters violate Indian airspace.

Operations Center 2, CIA Headquarters
Langley, Virginia

Morrison stormed into the room as Leroux stood, staring at the massive displays curving across the front of the state-of-the-art operations center located in the bowels of CIA Headquarters. "Report!" snapped the Chief.

Leroux indicated the displays. "They just retreated back across their border. It was just two fighters in formation that broke off too late. The other six that were with them managed not to cross."

"Are we saying this is an accident?"

"My gut's telling me it was completely intentional, but they'll claim it was an accident. But there's press all over that area. The BBC has a crew at the border, and they were in the middle of a live broadcast when it happened."

Randy Child, the team's tech wunderkind, spun in his chair. "I guess the Chinese won't be able to deny it happened then. Not that I expect them to deny it."

"What time is the facility supposed to open?" asked Morrison.

"Three PM local," replied Leroux. "The preliminaries start at two, then there's supposed to be an after-party."

Morrison pursed his lips as he stared at a replay of the shaky footage from a zoomed-in BBC camera showing the contrails of the two Chinese aircraft as they banked hard toward their own airspace. "What are they thinking?" he muttered.

"With this going on, do you really think he's going to be sticking around to sip champagne?" asked Child.

Morrison harumphed. "You don't know politicians. Any chance to press flesh while there are cameras around, well, you couldn't pry them out of there with a crowbar."

Leroux agreed. "At least we got them to switch his detour to be before the ceremony. That gets everyone out of the area that much quicker."

"Thank God for that." Morrison regarded Leroux. "Your gut's still telling you they're crossing the border?"

"Yes, and I suspect we'll see more of these airspace violations leading up to it. One of these times, none of them are going to turn back. The moment that happens, this is going down."

"And your assessment of the Indians' ability to repel them?"

"If the Chinese establish air superiority, little to none in the initial engagement. It's difficult terrain, so rapid progress by the Chinese forces won't be possible in great numbers. That should hopefully give the Indians time to get forces in position to prevent any serious penetration."

"But don't the Indians have defensive batteries like SAM sites?" asked Child. "Couldn't they just shoot down anything that crosses the border?"

"They do, and the Chinese know that because the Indians have been making a show of it to reassure their public…" Leroux's voice drifted off as something occurred to him.

Morrison eyed him. "What are you thinking?"

"I'm thinking that even if I establish overwhelming air superiority, I lose my propaganda dividend if I lose a lot of aircraft in the initial assault."

Morrison's eyebrows rose. "You think they're going to take out the SAM sites ahead of time?"

"If I were the Chinese and I knew I was absolutely crossing the border, I'd have Special Forces take out those SAM sites just before my planes crossed into their airspace. And by crossing into their airspace a few minutes ago, every single SAM site probably locked on, revealing their positions. I suspect very shortly we'll see more planes cross the border at different points to pick up any antiaircraft installations that weren't in range."

Child spun in his chair. "But if they're still just detecting where they are, is there enough time for them to position their people?"

Child was right. Everything was going down in the next few hours. The Chinese would need troops already in position, ready to destroy the known installations that couldn't simply be taken out by launching a missile across the border. Anything newly detected by the recent airspace violation, depending on the location, could be potentially targeted by missiles, however, if the Indians were being smart about it, which he had no doubt they were, any mobile site would have already been moved far enough making any acquired coordinates useless. The Chinese would need fresh troops to track down and destroy the new installations. If they attempted to insert troops, their choices were limited. They couldn't cross the border by land—the roads were controlled and the terrain too rough to traverse. They would have to do it by helicopter, but they would be easily detected. It would blow any element of surprise and push up their timeline, forcing them to take out the communications facility early, and kill an American senator.

An idea occurred to him and he spun toward Tong. "Bring up a list of every flight originating in China that will be passing through that area in the next hour."

One month from paradise

AD 1255

Oldamur woke to find a roof over his head. He couldn't recall the last time that had happened. Usually, he was greeted in the morning by the cloth of a tent, sometimes blue skies, and a pang of regret gripped him over the small luxury he had forgotten. He looked forward to reaching their new home where he could build a house for his family to once again enjoy the security four solid walls and a roof provided.

"You're awake."

He turned his head to see his wife sitting beside the bed he was in, smiling. "I am. Where am I?"

"You're in the village that we were trying to get to. When one of them heard of your heroism, they volunteered this room."

Everything came flooding back. The girl falling over the ledge, his attempted rescue, his broken leg. He sat upright and stared down at his legs, covered by a blanket. "My leg?"

"It's broken, but it has been set and splinted." She choked on the next words. "It could take months to heal."

He groaned. "Why did it have to be my leg? Anything but my leg. Break my arm and I could walk, but it had to my leg."

There was a knock at the door, and they both turned to see the mother and little girl standing there. "I'm sorry to disturb you, but she insisted on seeing you."

His wife leaned closer. "She's been sitting outside waiting for you to wake up this entire time."

He smiled at the little girl. "So, how are you doing?"

She shrugged, staring down at a bundle of flowers in her hands.

"Are those for me?"

She nodded rapidly.

He held out his hand. "May I see them?"

She hurried forward and thrust the flowers into his hands then jumped up on the bed and gave him a big hug. He grunted, the shifting of the weight sending a stabbing pain up his leg, but any hug from a child was worth it. He returned the embrace and she whispered in his ear. "Thank you for saving me. I'm sorry you got hurt."

He patted her on the back. "You're welcome."

She scrambled back to the floor and rejoined her mother, who stepped forward and clasped his hand in hers. She brought it to her mouth, giving it a kiss, her eyes glistening. "Thank you so much for saving my baby."

He patted her hands with his free one. "I did what any good man of faith would do."

She released his hands and glanced at his leg. "This is just so tragic. We were so close." Tears rolled down her cheeks. "If there's anything I can do, let me know." She smiled at Adelhaid before leaving the room.

Alone, Adelhaid sat on the edge of the bed. "She's right. We were so close. I don't know what we're going to do now."

His eyes narrowed. "What do you mean?"

"I mean, the group is moving on tomorrow, and there's no way you can travel. It'll be months before you're able to."

"You're going to go with them."

Her eyes shot wide. "We most certainly are not!"

He took her hand in his and smiled at her. "You must go with them, and when I'm well, I'll follow you. You heard Pierre. The path we're on now leads directly to our new home, but the journey could be dangerous. I want you and the children with the group. There's safety in numbers. When I'm healed, I'll come join you. I'll be able to travel quicker alone, so count the number of days it took to get there, add three months, and that's when you should see me."

"Leave you behind? Never!"

"You have to. I'll heal faster knowing that you and the children are safe, then perhaps we'll be able to shave a month off our separation. There's just one thing I ask."

"Anything, my love."

"By the time I get there, I expect you to have built us a fine home."

She giggled as the tears flowed. He reached up and wiped them away.

"Now, go get Pierre. We must finalize our plans so that we can be certain we'll see each other soon."

Skeleton Lake

Uttarakhand, India

Present Day

Acton stepped off the chopper and held out a hand, helping the others down onto the rock-strewn ground as the rotors continued to pound overhead. They had been concerned about continuing on with this visit, but their new embassy liaison—Jack nowhere to be found—assured them that everything was perfectly safe, and that the Chinese had already issued an apology for accidentally crossing the border. Reading had called bollocks on that, but when they were informed the senator would still be attending, they had agreed to continue—there was no way his security team would put him at risk, and everyone except Reading had agreed they shouldn't be intimidated by the Chinese.

The chopper lifted off and Reading gave his typical blunt assessment of the situation. "Well, this is rather disappointing, isn't it?"

Acton chuckled as he took in the scene. The lake that had come to be known as Skeleton Lake lay before them, and it wasn't much of a lake.

In fact, many might have simply called it a large pond. But there was evidence surrounding them that the body of water had once been much deeper and much larger. Accounts he had read of the area they now found themselves in described a sizeable glacier-fed lake with lush, green surroundings. What they were met with certainly wasn't that.

Somebody hailed them as the chopper cleared the canyon. Acton turned to see the senator walking toward them with half a dozen others.

"Professor Acton, I presume?"

Acton smiled and walked toward the man, his hand extended. "Senator Simmons. It's an honor, sir."

They clasped hands and Simmons gave a firm, vigorous shake. "The honor is mine, Professor. Thank you so much for indulging me. I'd like to introduce you to Professor Jagmeet Sharma. He's in charge of the Indian group of scientists studying the area."

"Jagmeet?" exclaimed Laura, rushing forward.

"Laura Palmer? What are you doing here?"

Laura embraced Sharma, then stepped back, jerking a thumb toward Acton. "I married this bum."

Sharma laughed and extended a hand toward Acton. "I would hardly call one of the most preeminent archaeologists in the world a bum."

Acton shook his hand. "I've been called worse. Hell, *she's* called me worse."

Sharma laughed. "She is not one to mince words. I was so pleased when I heard it would be you accompanying the senator. I had no idea, however, I'd get the added bonus of seeing my old friend."

"How do you know each other?"

"I studied at University College London some time ago, back when Laura was just starting out as a professor."

"Jagmeet was one of my best students." She waved an arm at the area. "I see you're doing well for yourself."

He smiled. "It's a small team with a smaller budget, but we're doing good work." His eyes twinkled with mischief as he turned to Acton. "Tell me, Professor, what's your first impression?"

"Certainly not what the brochure promised."

Sharma laughed. "No, it's not much to look at anymore, is it?"

"What happened?" asked Reading.

Acton made quick introductions before Sharma replied. "As you can see, the lake used to be much bigger. It was glacier-fed and still is to a small extent. If you look at this large deposit of rocks surrounding the area, it leaves very little room for vegetation to grow—certainly not any lush paradise that has been described in some ancient texts." He pointed up at the mountain to the east of them. "What we believe happened is a glacier that was once on this mountain collapsed about two-hundred years ago. There could have been a large lake above caused by an extended warming period, and when the warming caused melting underneath the glacier, the speed at which it was moving down the mountain increased, perhaps breaking the basin the lake had been formed in. This would have sent a massive rush of water, ice, and collected debris down the side of the mountain. It essentially turned what was once a lush valley into a wasteland."

Acton frowned as he surveyed the area. "Paradise lost."

"It would seem so."

Simmons stepped toward the edge of the lake. "So, the bones that are in here could have been from people who were living here and got caught up in this flood or avalanche or whatever you want to call it?"

"Some, possibly, but the problem with that theory is that we have carbon dated bones from this lake, and they date over a period of nearly one thousand years. If it had been a single cataclysmic event, they'd all date from the same era, but they don't. That means the bodies somehow made it into the lake over centuries."

"Some sort of burial ritual?"

"It's a definite possibility, however, many of the bones we've been able to examine show signs of blunt force trauma. Many of these people died horrible deaths. Now it could be that the bodies were brought here from other locations, victims of massacres over the centuries. But as I suspect you're already aware, Senator, the age of the bones isn't the only mystery here. It's the origins."

Simmons grinned. "You caught me, Professor. Ever since I read bones that could only belong to Europeans were found here, I realized there must be more to the story."

"Oh, there's definitely more to the story, Senator. However, you'll be disappointed to hear that we know little of what that story might be." He raised a finger. "However, we made a remarkable discovery only a week ago that may shed a little bit of light on what happened here during the past millennium."

This piqued Acton's curiosity. Before arriving, he had read everything he could find, including all the latest research, but nothing mentioned any significant discovery in years. He took Laura's hand, sensing her own excitement.

"Well, Jagmeet, what did you find?" she asked eagerly.

Sharma smiled then indicated the rockface behind them. "I think it's better to show you, but I must warn you"—he glanced at the youngest of their companions—"what you're about to see is both tragic and disturbing."

Tommy gulped and glanced at Mai, who shrugged. "There's no way I'm not seeing this."

Tommy didn't appear as certain, though concurred. "We're good."

"Very well." Sharma led them toward the rockface where a hive of activity was contained behind bright yellow tape.

"Police tape?" asked Acton.

Sharma groaned. "You would not believe what we have to contend with here. So many tourists come through, and they think it's their right to just take the bones. I keep petitioning the government to let us close off the entire valley so we can preserve it as a heritage site, but nobody seems to care. At least half of what was here is gone now, sitting in living rooms around the world, a macabre trophy of someone's visit to the mystical land of India, no doubt acting as a bookend to an English translation of the Kama Sutra."

Laura smirked at him. "I don't remember you being so cynical."

Sharma grunted. "They're no better than grave robbers."

Acton held up the tape so the others could duck under it. "Well, there's a difference. Grave robbers know what they're doing. These people are just idiots."

"Yes, I suppose so, but my word, how do so many idiots know how to book a plane ticket?" He paused at the entrance, several of his team stepping aside. "We discovered this last week quite by accident. There was a bit of a landslide that revealed it." He pointed at the stone overhead, still containing a large amount of loose rock. "And I have to warn you, there could be another landslide at any time, which is why we put emergency supplies inside. There's food, water, emergency lights—enough that you'll be able to last several days with no problem, and we'll have you out by then. But like I said, there is a risk. Are you certain you want to proceed?"

Acton didn't hesitate. "Absolutely." He turned back to Simmons. "The risk is real, Senator. Perhaps it might be best if you stayed outside."

One of Simmons' security personnel stepped forward. "I think Professor Acton is correct, sir."

Simmons rolled his eyes. "My head of security, Rick Bradley. Always overprotective." He dismissed his concerns with a flick of his wrist and stepped toward the entrance. "If terrorists can't stop me from going to church, rocks won't stop me from going inside." He winked at Acton. "Fortune favors the bold."

Acton slapped the man on the back. "And sometimes the stupid. Let's go." He let Sharma lead the way, and once they were inside, he blinked rapidly, his vision slowly adjusting to the reduced light.

"Don't walk forward until you can see clearly. You might step on something."

Several lights ahead shone toward them, casting long shadows on the ground, confusing things, but soon Acton was sure enough of his footing

98

to move forward. Sharma led them in about ten yards then turned, holding up his hands. They all gathered in front of him and he pointed toward the edges. "Tell me what you see."

Acton turned and his eyebrows shot up. They were surrounded by skeletons, most of them against the walls in seated positions, some horizontal as if lying at the feet of the others or in the laps of those still upright, tattered clothing still adorning them.

"Bloody hell," muttered Reading. "What the devil happened here?"

"Our theory is that these people lived in this cave. When we go deeper, you'll see distinct living areas where family groups lived, but these clothes suggest they died a couple of hundred years ago. We don't have carbon dating results back yet, but I suspect they'll date to the most recent bones we found in the lake."

Acton slowly rounded the area, examining the remains without touching, Laura and Simmons doing the same. Acton swirled a finger at their surroundings. "This isn't a living space. These people were waiting here for something."

"Very good, Professor," said Sharma. "We've had a little more time to think about it, and we've seen what's deeper inside, but our going theory is that anyone who was outside at the beginning of the glacier collapse likely rushed in here to escape what they saw coming down the mountain, only to be trapped inside. There are stones piled deeper inside that we believe were taken from the entrance to make room for the escape efforts, but there was simply too much, and before they could get out, they ran out of air."

Tommy shifted uncomfortably. "If they couldn't save themselves, what makes you think we can?"

Simmons put a comforting hand on Tommy's shoulder, giving him a gentle shake. "Because, young man, we have modern equipment and people working from the outside."

Acton regarded Tommy and Mai. This situation was sketchy, and if he were running the dig site, he wouldn't have this opened yet, not without safety measures in place. He had no doubt, if it weren't for who Sharma's guests were, he wouldn't have been so accommodating. Acton was certain the man had received a phone call from New Delhi ordering him to pull out all the stops when it came to the senator's visit. He pointed ahead. "How about you show us what else you found? We'll take a quick look then get back outside where everyone can be more comfortable."

"Absolutely," agreed Sharma, who led them deeper into what turned out to be a cave network, carved out over thousands upon thousands of years by the glacier meltwaters overhead. The channel they were in took a sharp bend to the right, then opened up into a massive chamber, and everyone, including Reading, gasped. Dozens of battery-powered portable lights lit the area, revealing the rest of Sharma's team painstakingly documenting what was an incredible find. Scores of skeletons were visible, and distinct sleeping areas surrounded the outer edge. Personal belongings were carefully laid out, some on stone slabs, some in alcoves carved into the stone.

"How many?" asked Laura, her tone reverent.

"Over two hundred, with an unusually large number of children."

100

"Interesting." Acton walked over to one of the family units. "You would think, with limited space like this, they would try to keep the birthrate down."

"Would they have understood things like that back then?" asked Tommy. "It's not like they could pop out to 7-Eleven and grab a pack of Jimmies."

Mai snickered and Acton laughed, the entire chamber echoing. Acton snapped his jaw shut as the first report clapped back at him, embarrassed at the disrespect he had just shown in what was a tomb to an entire community. "Sorry," he said to those in the chamber.

Tommy appeared crestfallen. "It's my fault, Professor. I shouldn't have made a joke."

Sharma patted him on the shoulder. "There's no need to apologize. Even I've been guilty of enjoying myself in here. It's easy to forget what this represents, especially when one loves their work so much. This is the find of a lifetime. We could spend years here documenting everything. It could revolutionize our thinking on just what Skeleton Lake represents."

"Have you found any written texts yet?" asked Simmons.

Sharma shook his head. "Not yet, but right now we're only—"

"Do you feel that?" interrupted Mai.

Acton turned to her. "Feel what?"

"It feels like a vibration."

Acton tensed then crouched, placing his hand on the cold stone of the cave floor. The vibrations were unmistakable. He shot to his feet and pointed at the exit. "Everybody out, now!"

What was causing it was irrelevant—vibrations like this could shake loose the stone above the entrance. Simmons' bodyguard Bradley grabbed him by the arm without hesitation, leading the man down the tunnel toward safety. Reading took charge of Tommy and Mai as Acton turned to Laura.

"Get out now!"

She joined him at the entrance to the chamber. "I'm staying with you."

"I need someone with a level head out there in case things go bad. Go!"

She thankfully didn't argue, and instead headed into the tunnel after giving him a peck on the cheek as the vibrations grew. Sharma urged his team to hurry and Acton beckoned them toward the exit when he noticed dust falling from above. A crash deeper in the cave had several of the team crying out in fear as they picked their way toward safety. Another stalactite broke free overhead and shattered onto the surface below, sending debris in every direction. Acton grabbed the hand of a panicked woman, helping her the final few feet toward the tunnel that led to the exit, then as the last cleared, he and Sharma followed them through, the rumble growing.

"What the hell is it?" asked Acton.

Sharma shook his head. "I don't know. Nothing like this has happened in the entire time we've been here. It almost feels like an earthquake."

Acton disagreed. "An earthquake wouldn't last this long. Something else is causing this."

They rounded a bend and daylight shone ahead. Acton breathed a sigh of relief at the knowledge the opening was still clear, but as they neared, he cursed at the sight of stones falling in front of them. "Hurry!" he shouted. "And cover your heads!" Those ahead of them raised their arms, clasping them around their heads as they crouched forward, surging through to the outside.

"James, hurry!" begged Laura.

Sharma stumbled, falling to his knees. Acton reached out and grabbed him, pulling him back to his feet then toward the entrance, shoving him through the opening then covering his head as he leaped after him. He hit the ground hard but forced himself to roll as stone from above continued to rain down behind him. He scrambled to his feet and grabbed Sharma lying beside him, then sprinted down the slippery slope toward the lake and safety where the others had already gathered. He quickly did a headcount of his own people and spun toward Sharma.

"Headcount!"

"Everyone is accounted for," replied a gasping Sharma as he visibly made a second count just to be certain. "Did anyone get injured?"

A young man raised his hand, blood trickling down it. "I got hit by a rock. I'll be all right."

Acton turned toward Simmons. "Senator, are you all right?"

Simmons brushed the dust off his clothes, his eyes wide with excitement. "I am fine, Professor. And I'm shocked to report that so is my underwear. I think that's the most scared I've ever been in my life."

Acton chuckled and everyone turned back toward the cave to see a pile of stones now partially blocked the entrance, and the rocks continued to fall. In all the excitement, he had forgotten the cause, and finally noticed that the vibrations continued. He turned, scanning the area, his heart leaping into his throat as Tommy pointed toward the makeshift road that led into the valley.

"Look!"

A convoy of military vehicles rumbled toward them, including a menacing-looking tracked vehicle, the likely source of the vibrations that had nearly buried them alive. The weapons platform, mounted on top, appeared to be a missile battery.

Reading stepped up beside him. "Please tell me that's Indian military and not Chinese."

Acton squinted then spotted a flag mounted to the rear of one of the vehicles and breathed a sigh of relief. "They're Indian."

"Thank God," muttered Laura as she took his hand.

A jeep surged ahead, racing toward them. Simmons' security team reached for their weapons but the senator urged calm. "Let's just see what they want. Remember, they are our allies."

The vehicle skidded to a halt on the loose stone and an officer hopped out of the passenger seat, saying something in Hindi. Sharma raised his hand and stepped forward.

"I'm in charge here. May we speak English so my guests can understand?"

The officer nodded. "Your guests aren't Indian?"

Sharma shook his head and extended a hand toward Simmons. "This is United States Senator Joseph Simmons."

The officer's eyes bulged for a moment and he snapped to attention. "Senator, it is an honor to meet you. I am Major Singh of the Indian Armed Forces. It's not safe for you to be here."

Simmons stepped forward and extended a hand. "And why is that, Major?"

Singh shook the hand then returned to his stiff pose. "We're setting up a mobile Surface-to-Air missile battery in this valley. Should something go wrong, this could become a primary target. I highly recommend everyone leaves here immediately."

Sharma eyed the man. "Is that an order?"

"Not for you, sir, but for the foreign nationals, yes."

Simmons raised a hand. "No problem. We were just about to leave regardless."

"I'm pleased to hear that, Senator." Singh pointed toward the road they had just arrived on. "When you reach the main road, turn right. That will take you west, away from the danger."

Simmons shook his head. "I'm sorry, Major, but we'll be going east. We are attending the official opening of the new communications facility."

Singh frowned. "How are you getting there?"

Simmons pointed toward two SUVs parked several hundred yards away.

"No armed escort?"

Simmons shook his head. "It wasn't felt like it was necessary."

Singh scratched his chin. "It probably isn't. At least not yet. If you are indeed attending the opening, my briefing suggested the Chinese weren't going to do anything until after it was opened. Your journey there should be safe, however, Senator, I highly recommend the moment it's over, you get yourselves out of the area as quickly as possible."

"Sage advice, Major, advice we all intend to heed." Simmons turned to Sharma. "I'm afraid I don't have the authority to invite you to the ceremony as it's a military facility and only those on the guest list will be allowed in. Besides, we'll be leaving by helicopter when it's over so there's no room for your team. Do you have a way of getting out of the area?"

Sharma gestured toward the other vehicles parked with the SUVs. "We'll be fine, Senator, though we have no intention of leaving here. At least not yet."

Laura took Sharma by the arm. "Jagmeet, you have to go now. You're responsible for all these people."

Sharma smiled. "You don't understand. In the three years I've been here, I've lost count of how many times we've been told by military patrols that there could be trouble with China and that we should leave immediately. It never comes to pass. Just like this time, it's much ado about nothing. The Chinese will make their noise. India shall make hers. Statements will be made for consumption by the masses, then everyone will return to the negotiating table. It's nothing we haven't seen a hundred times before, and I'm sure we'll be seeing a hundred times again. There can never be peace with China in its current state, and I for one will not allow them to disrupt my life."

Simmons smiled, patting Sharma on the upper arm. "Well said, my friend. No one should yield to terror."

Laura lowered her voice, leaning closer to Sharma. "At least give your people the choice. Some of them look pretty scared to me."

Sharma surveyed his team then indicated Singh. "You heard what the major said. If any of you want to leave now, I understand perfectly, and nothing will be said. When the crisis is over, you'll be welcomed back with no judgment and no damage to your career or future on this project. I will be remaining, but that is my choice alone. If anyone wants to remain with me, they are welcome, and if not, please make your decision now."

The mix of students and seasoned team members broke into several groups, hushed conversations had, and within moments, over half were heading toward the vehicles, each shaking their professor's hand as they left, some with tears, all making their apologies. As the two cars carrying the departing members drove out of sight, Sharma turned to Laura and Acton. "I'll be honest. I didn't expect that many to leave," he whispered.

Acton gestured toward the anti-aircraft battery being set up. "In all your time here, has anything like this happened?"

Sharma sighed. "No, I suppose it hasn't."

Laura leaned even closer. "Your team is scared."

Sharma chewed his cheek for a moment before he turned to her. "What would you do?"

"You won't like what I'm going to say, Jagmeet, but I would get everybody in the vehicles now and leave. If it turns out to be nothing, you come back tomorrow, but if it turns into something, you're out of the line of fire"—she jabbed a finger toward the missile battery—"because *that* is going to be a primary target. The Chinese will hit that with a bomb big enough to take out this entire area, and if any of your people are inside that cave, they'll be condemned to death, because even if they could be rescued, there will be no one to do the rescuing because the Chinese could be all over this area. The team that just left will come back when this is all over, and they'll be documenting *your* remains."

Sharma's jaw clenched as his head slowly bobbed. Finally, a burst of air escaped his lips and he gave a curt nod. "You're right." He turned to the remaining team members. "Grab whatever you don't want to leave behind. We're leaving until this crisis is over."

The relieved expressions revealed that those who had remained behind weren't doing it from a lack of concern, but out of a sense of loyalty to their professor or worry over their careers. They scattered toward a nearby camp and a relieved major shook Sharma's hand, saying something in Hindi. Singh turned to Simmons and saluted him.

"Senator, it's an honor to have met you. Safe journey."

Simmons bowed his head. "Thank you, Major. You, your men, and your country are in our prayers."

Singh snapped out a bow. "Thank you, Senator." The man turned on his heel and headed back toward his troops, one of them shaking a map and yelling something, leaving Acton to wonder if the soldiers were in the correct location.

Bradley cleared his throat. "Senator, we should leave immediately."

"Yes, of course." Simmons extended his hand toward the remaining vehicles. "Shall we?"

Bradley led the way as the Indians continued to set up their weapon system and establish a security perimeter. Everyone climbed in their assigned SUVs and the driver introduced himself as Veer before getting them underway, Simmons' vehicle taking the lead. They drove in silence, the mood somber, though their near-death experience was the furthest thing from Acton's mind. His concern now was whether the people he felt responsible for were safe.

As he stared out the window, his head pressed against the glass, something caught his eye and he tilted his head upward. "What the hell is that?"

Operations Center 2, CIA Headquarters

Langley, Virginia

Leroux stared at the display as scores of flights scrolled by, all meeting the criteria he had given Tong. "We need to narrow that down. Cross-reference that list with the airline database. Eliminate anything that has at least ten or more passengers from a NATO country."

"Give me a second," replied Tong as her fingers flew over the keyboard. The manifest of all international flights was required to be shared with any jurisdiction the airline might enter. This included passport numbers, the list of which were constantly analyzed for anything suspicious—expired passports, stolen passports, or duplicates. Tong hit a key and leaned back. "Got it."

Leroux stared at the screen and smiled. "Three flights."

"That's a little bit easier," commented Child. "Now what?"

"Trackback those flights to see where they came from, see where they're supposed to be going, and if they're actually following their flight plan. And see if we have satellite footage of them."

"What are we looking for?" asked Tong.

"You'll know it when you see it."

Marc Therrien, one of his senior analysts, cursed from the back of the room. "Well, I see it and I think I know it."

Leroux spun in his chair and Therrien pointed at the displays. "Putting it up now. How the hell you thought of this, I have no idea."

Leroux turned and smiled at the image, giddy with the knowledge he had been right, then sick at what it meant. He headed for the door, pointing at the display. "Send that footage to the Chief. I'm going to go see him now. And send an analysis to my phone. Every detail you can glean. And keep looking at those other planes and start backtracking twenty-four hours at a time. Use the same search criteria. We need to find out how long they've been doing this."

"We're on it," replied Tong as Leroux pushed through the secure doors and sprinted for the elevators, his heart hammering.

They were already at war.

Only nobody knew it.

Enroute to Indian Army Northern Command Communications Center

Uttarakhand, India

Acton rolled his window down and shoved his head out, twisting it to see the sky overhead. What at first appeared to be large birds soared overhead, but they weren't birds at all—they were people, dangling under deployed parachute canopies. "Do you see that?"

"See what?" asked Reading from the front seat.

"Those skydivers."

Reading rolled down his window and stuck his head out. "I don't see any…wait, there they are."

"I'm not seeing things, right? Those are skydivers, right?"

Reading nodded. "Those are definitely skydivers." He turned to the driver, Veer. "Do you guys have skydivers here? Paragliders? Anything like that?"

Veer shook his head. "Not that I'm aware of, and I'm certain anything like that would be grounded with what's going on."

Reading cursed and reached over, honking the horn three times then shoving an arm out the window, pointing at the sky. Bradley leaned out his window a moment later and looked up before shouting something. The lead SUV suddenly accelerated, Bradley waving his hand for them to follow. Veer hammered on the gas and Reading rolled up his window as Acton continued to watch at least a dozen people dropping from the sky. He pulled out his phone and took dozens of photos in rapid succession before recording a short video. He handed the device over to Tommy, their resident expert.

"See what you can pick up on that. We need to know who they are."

Tommy took the phone and connected it to his laptop, the images rapidly downloading. "I doubt we're going to be able to tell who they are, sir. Everything is too far away to see faces, and we definitely won't be able to make out any insignia."

"Soldiers would be wearing some sort of camouflage. Tourists and teams tend to wear bright colors. Let's at least figure out that part of the equation."

Tommy pressed his thumb and forefinger against the laptop screen then spread them. "Looks like some sort of camouflage blend, all in the light and dark grays." He zoomed in on another image. "Looks like they're all wearing the same thing."

Reading cursed as did Acton while Tommy showed everyone the images.

"I think we can safely assume they're military," said Acton.

Reading agreed. "But whose?"

Laura pressed her head against the glass. "And why are they here?"

Reading gripped the dash as they took a hard right. "I think we can assume they're Chinese. I can't see any reason for the Indians to insert troops like that."

"But wouldn't the Indians have seen the aircraft that they jumped from?" asked Mai.

Acton shook his head. "Not if they did a HAHO jump."

Tommy stared at him. "Huh?"

"High Altitude High Opening. You basically jump from a very high altitude with oxygen, then open high so you maximize your hangtime. It allows you to cover a lot of horizontal distance. They could definitely make it from the Chinese border to here."

Tommy's eyes narrowed. "So, they're probably a Special Forces unit?"

"Probably, which means we don't want to run into them."

Reading smashed a fist against the dash. "Every bloody time something has to go wrong. Just once, I'd like to go somewhere in the world where someone isn't trying to kill us."

Acton shrugged. "I don't think anybody would buy that book."

Reading growled at him. "This is no time for joking."

Acton checked his phone and cursed. "Does anybody have a signal?"

Phones were checked and heads shook all around.

"What about the satphone?" asked Mai.

Laura shook her head. "Like a fool, I left it with our luggage. I assumed since we were with the senator's people, we would have good communications. And I certainly never thought we'd need a phone because Chinese paratroopers were dropping on our heads."

Reading glanced back at her. "With you two, you should always assume the worst. Next time you see Dylan, ask him if there's some sort of communications device you can have implanted into your skull. You two could use it."

Tommy grinned. "That would be so cool."

Acton rolled his eyes. "I'll let Elon know you're ready for a Neuralink implant."

"Show's what you know. I already applied to be a test subject."

Mai smacked him. "You did what?"

Laura gave them both a look. "I think you two can discuss this later, don't you?"

Mai agreed, though maintained her cold stare at her boyfriend. "We are *definitely* discussing this later."

Tommy grimaced as he leaned away from the woman he loved, who at that moment appeared more dangerous than the Chinese dangling above them.

"Hey, I see a parachute!" said Veer as he leaned forward, staring up at the sky.

"Keep your eyes on the bloody road!" snapped Reading.

Acton peered out the window again and saw the paratroopers were approaching the ground. "Let's see where they're landing," he said as he ducked back inside. "We can report their position to the Indians once we reach the communications facility."

"Bollocks! We're keeping that accelerator pressed to the floor, we're getting our asses to that facility, then onto a chopper back to New Delhi." Reading twisted in his seat so he could see them all. "Agreed?"

115

Acton wanted to do more but Reading was right. Their responsibility wasn't to put their lives at risk to gather intel for the Indian military. Their duty was to themselves. Get to safety, report what they saw, then get the hell out of Dodge.

Heads bobbed around the cabin as everyone concurred.

"Good," said Reading, relieved. "Now that the nonsense is out of the way, see if you can get our exact position on that tablet and mark where we think they're landing. India may no longer be the jewel in the crown, but there's no way in hell I want the bloody Chinese running roughshod over it."

Director Morrison's Office, CIA Headquarters

Langley, Virginia

Leroux was buzzed through to Morrison's office and he stumbled inside, gasping for breath as the Chief leaned back in his chair, folding his arms.

"How can a guy as slim as you be so out of shape?"

Leroux sucked in several lungsful of air, holding up a finger, indicating his boss would have to wait for a reply. He dropped into the chair in front of Morrison's desk and thrust his shoulders back, opening his chest cavity so he could take deeper breaths. "I'm blessed with my mother's metabolism that allows me to eat anything I want, and my father's enthusiasm for sitting."

Morrison chuckled. "I'm just looking at this footage your team sent. I assume this is what I think it is."

"If you think it's footage of the Chinese inserting troops across the border using HAHO jumps, then yes."

"How many?"

Leroux wagged his phone. "The last update I received was the one aircraft inserted three teams of twelve. I've got my people backtracking though, a day at a time, to see if other teams were inserted."

"Well, it appears you might have been second to the punch."

"Sir?"

Morrison leaned forward and tapped on his laptop. "I just got a flash update. The senator's security team spotted the same paratroops being inserted into their area."

Leroux tensed. "Are they safe?"

Morrison threw up his hands. "Who the hell knows? When the message was received, yes. They were almost at the communications facility, and once there, they should be safe. For the moment."

"I assume they're going to evac immediately?"

"You would assume that, but you'd be wrong."

"Excuse me?"

"You'd be wrong. Apparently, when the senator's security team reported what they saw, it was during a video conference between our people and the Indians. They admitted they were aware the Chinese had been inserting troops using this method for several days."

Leroux's eyebrows shot up. "And they did nothing about it?"

"No, they actually brought in Special Forces and claim they pinpointed the positions of all the Chinese teams. They don't want to cancel the ceremony because they're afraid it will tip their hand."

Butterflies launched inside Leroux's stomach as he realized what was being said. "So, they want us to pretend our people didn't see what they did, and go on with the ceremony as if nothing's happened?"

"Exactly. They want time to locate these new teams."

Leroux checked his watch. "But the ceremony starts in less than two hours. Do they really think there's enough time?"

"That's not for us to say. Personally, no, I don't think it's enough time, not with the difficulties of moving in that region. This latest team has been put in last minute in the vicinity of the communications facility for a reason."

"You don't think they're going to assault the compound with troops, do you?"

"No, though they might be there to lase the target or to assess bomb damage."

Leroux's head slowly bobbed. "Do you think the Chinese will take it out without any warning?"

Morrison tilted his head slightly. "That's one of the debates raging at the White House right now. The smart move would be to provide a warning, to give the Indians perhaps fifteen minutes to evacuate their personnel. The Chinese can launch missiles from their side of the border and take out that facility with little problem and no risk to themselves. If they don't provide a warning, a lot of people are going to die, and that blood is on Chinese hands. It would make them appear the aggressor, and if I'm the Indians, I'm going to make sure that every newscast is running with footage of mangled corpses. The optics wouldn't be good for them."

Leroux frowned, scratching his chin. "I'm not so sure they're concerned about optics. Soldiers dying while serving their country isn't something I think they'd necessarily worry about. They've already given their warning. They've said when the facility opens, they're taking it out. If the Indians choose to ignore that, the Chinese will view that as acceptance of whatever casualties may come from that decision. The only delay I think we can count on is them waiting for the senator to leave."

Morrison pursed his lips as he regarded him. "I think you're right, but either way, that facility is getting hit in the next several hours."

"And the senator is aware of all of this?"

"He's been made aware and has indicated he's delivering his speech, and I quote, 'No damn Chinese dictator is going to prevent the public from hearing what I have to say.'"

Leroux grunted. "Brave words if you were anyone else at that event, not so much when you know you're the only person there the Chinese can't touch. If he were truly brave, he'd volunteer to stick around for a few days."

"Don't be too hard on the man. You know politics is optics. I've met him many times, and I truly believe in situations like this he thinks he's doing the right thing. It's the press and his team that will spin this in his favor. If he gives his speech, leaves, and five minutes later that installation blows up, he won't be worrying about his reelection bid. He'll be the American hero that the Chinese tried to kill."

"And what about the professors? Will they be made aware?"

Morrison shook his head. "No. And they are not to be. The White House doesn't want anyone making a scene and disrupting what's planned."

Leroux's jaw clenched for a moment. "That hardly seems fair."

"I agree, which is why I implemented a failsafe."

Paradise

AD 1255

Adelhaid gasped as they rounded a bend in the path they had been following for so long. It opened into a large valley, mountains surrounding them, but inside sat an oasis with a glistening lake surrounded by green grass, shrubs, and trees. It was idyllic.

It was paradise.

She rushed up to Pierre. "Is this it? Is this our new home?"

"This is indeed your final resting place," he confirmed as he continued to walk deeper into the valley.

"Mother, it's beautiful!" cried Zaleska as her daughter slammed into her side, wrapping her arms around her mother. Adelhaid patted Zaleska's back as Ajtony joined them.

"Is this our new home, Mother?"

"I think it is." She took a moment to survey their surroundings and her eyes narrowed. Where were the people? Where were those they were supposed to join?

Pierre continued forward in front of them then he turned and raised his hands. The large group surrounded the man by the lake's edge, shouting dozens of questions. He raised his hands again to calm the crowd. All eyes were now on the man who had brought them so far.

"Children! I want you to gather around me. What I have to say is for you."

Adelhaid gripped her children closer as they were only paces away from the man.

"We have finally reached the end of your journey, and I know you have many questions. I shall explain everything to you, but you must let me speak without interruptions. You have all heard my story of how my family was betrayed by the Church and ruined by the indulgences required to save the souls of my father and grandfather." Heads bobbed throughout the crowd, including Adelhaid's. Oldamur had told her the story, a story so close to their own, it had been one of the reasons they had decided they could trust the man. "I have a confession to make. That wasn't my story to tell. That was the story of a man I barely knew, and while true, it is not my own."

Adelhaid gasped, and she wasn't the only one. Why would he lie about such a thing? Her stomach churned as an unease took hold.

"I'm sure you're asking yourself why I would claim this story as my own, but there was a reason." He stepped forward and placed his hand atop one of the children. "I was once one of you. One of the innocent children. My parents brought me here, escaping the problems they had created, tearing me away from everything I had known, everyone I had loved, all because they had made a mess of their lives. The man who led these pilgrimages before me, described this place much as I did—a paradise where one could leave all their problems behind and start over, living in harmony.

"But think about it, children. If you got in trouble, and were told that all you had to do so that you weren't punished was to leave everything you knew, to leave your family and friends, your home, your farm, would you do it? Or would you accept the consequences of your actions, and admit that you had made a mistake, and that you had to make it right? I think deep down you all know what the correct answer is. You would accept whatever punishment your parents decided was necessary to teach you a lesson, you would learn that lesson, then continue your life with your family. Yet, that's not what your parents did. Your parents made mistakes, and your parents ran away from their problems.

"But for many of them, the problems still exist. Many have left behind debts that their families are now forced to pay, your grandmothers and grandfathers, your aunts and uncles, your cousins, will all suffer because of the choice your parents made. Now I ask you, does that seem right?"

Several children shook their heads, and Adelhaid was dismayed to see both her children agreed with Pierre.

"My parents made the same wicked choice and followed my predecessor here to this paradise, for it is a paradise. But just like the Kingdom of Heaven, one must be worthy to gain entry. And I'm afraid only you children are worthy."

"Just what are you saying?" asked a man, his voice angry, though tinged with fear. "Are you saying we came all this way for nothing? That you're not going to keep your promise?"

Pierre regarded the man. "I am keeping my promise. If you'll recall, I said that this paradise was open to all who were worthy. In your arrogance, you assumed you were. This pilgrimage was not to save you from your torments, it was to save your children from your sins."

"But what do you mean? You're older than I am, yet you get to live here? How is that fair?"

Pierre frowned, shaking his head. "Nowhere have I heard that our time on this Earth would be fair, or even should be fair. We live the best lives we can here, then go to whatever Heaven or afterlife we believe in. Only there, should we be judged worthy, is life fair. But you are confused. I was never an adult like you. I was a victim of my parents and was saved by these people years ago. They raised me, taught me everything I needed to know, kept me clothed and fed and warm."

Adelhaid could hold her tongue no longer. "What people do you speak of? There's no one here."

Pierre chuckled and waved his hand toward the mountain behind them. "You are mistaken, my friend. We are many. We are the Children of the Lake, and like our ancestors have done for generations, we continue the duty handed down to us. We save the children from the sinners."

Adelhaid turned to look behind her and gasped. Hundreds surrounded them. Men and women, some her age, some old enough to be her grandparents, and peppered among them were children of all ages.

And almost all of them had a weapon.

She gripped her children tight against her, turning back to Pierre. "Please, just let us go! We won't tell anybody about this place. We swear!"

124

Pierre leaned back and laughed. "You have no idea how many times I've heard that same promise. What you must realize is that this is a moment to rejoice. Your children will live in a paradise free of the burdens their parents suffered, content with the knowledge that their parents were absolved of their sins, no matter how egregious, because they died in a futile attempt to save their children."

The crowds surrounding them roared and her children screamed. She grabbed them each by a hand and pulled them toward the water, away from the group. If they could swim across the lake, they might get away and return down the path that had brought them here. But her first step into the water felled those hopes, the biting cold of the glacier-fed lake brutal. Screams and cries continued behind her, but she dared not look, for the horror of it would overwhelm her and she had to think straight.

To their right was the mountain pass they had come through. Her only hope was to reach it before those battling on the shore noticed. Both of her children were sobbing, despite her urges for them to remain quiet. The chance of them being heard over the massacre behind them, however, were slim. She dragged them through the ice-cold water, her legs quickly numbing. Her foot came down on something hard and it rolled like a log beneath her. She collapsed and the frigid water swallowed her entire body. She struggled to regain her footing and flipped over onto her stomach before opening her eyes.

And what she saw littering the lake bottom had her screaming out whatever air was left in her lungs.

Indian Army Northern Command Communications Center

Uttarakhand, India

Present Day

Acton breathed a sigh of relief as they were waved through the gates, putting them securely behind the fence that surrounded the installation. They drove up a winding road as they all took in their surroundings. It was rather underwhelming. For all the ado made about the opening of this communications facility, he was expecting something far more impressive than what he now saw. The building was small. A Burger King might fit inside. The array of satellite dishes and antennae were impressive, but the true hero of the hour was the setting. The back of the structure sat against a cliff face that jutted skyward and out of sight. There was evidence of recent blasting, the cliff scarred with piles of rubble strewn outside the concrete pad they now found themselves driving on.

The pad was jam-packed with vehicles, some military, most civilian. A single helicopter sat on the roof of the structure, and if it was meant to take them and the senator's team out, it didn't appear large enough for the task. Veer came to a halt and several soldiers in dress uniform stepped forward, their white gloves gripping the door handles before letting them out in unison.

"Professor Acton!"

Acton glanced over his shoulder to see Simmons waving at him from the doorway.

"I need to have a word with you."

They all headed toward the man but Simmons shook his head. "Just you, Professor. You're my official guest."

Acton turned to the others. "Just give me a moment. I'll see what he wants."

"Bollocks." Reading's face was red. "This concerns all of us."

"I agree, however, the senator wants to speak with me, and he should know full well that the moment he's out of my sight, I'm telling you everything he said. Now, just stay here and try not to retake India in the name of the British Empire just because you're pissed off at our situation."

"It's too bloody hot. We should have stayed out of Asia."

Acton gave him a look. "The only reason you're hot is because it's under your collar. It's beautiful here right now."

Reading glared at him for a moment before finally noticing the cool mountain air surrounding them. "Actually, this isn't too bad. Did anyone bring a Union Jack?"

Laura rolled her eyes. "Go see what the senator wants and I'll keep his pride holstered."

127

Tommy snickered.

Mai smacked him.

Acton grinned. "When we get home, we're going to review all the euphemisms for penis that us Yanks have."

Her jaw dropped in shock and he turned, heading over to the senator, who by now was growing impatient.

"Sorry, Senator, but there was some debate on who should be told what."

Simmons gave a quick flick of the wrist, dismissing the apology. "No time for that. This is the situation. Apparently, the Indians are aware that the Chinese have been inserting troops, like those you spotted earlier. They have assured us that they're dealing with the situation, but that if we call off our participation in the ceremony, it might make the Chinese suspicious and they could act sooner than planned. The White House has left the choice up to me, and I've decided I'm going to give my speech."

Acton shifted uncomfortably. "With all due respect, Senator, I don't think you can make that decision on our behalf."

Simmons smiled slightly. "You are absolutely correct, Professor. And if it were just your lives at stake, we would all be leaving, but we could be looking at thousands, perhaps even millions of lives that could be lost if we give in to the Chinese today. You have to look at the bigger picture here. Today, we're drawing a line in the sand. If the Chinese choose to cross it, a price will have to be paid."

"By them or us?"

"Unfortunately, Professor, in war, a price is paid by all."

LAKE OF BONES

Acton glared at him. "Senator, did you have any idea when you invited me that this was the situation you were dragging me and the others into?"

Simmons shook his head. "I promise you, Professor, while I knew the situation was tense, I had no idea how far things would go."

"Yet I don't see your wife here."

Simmons flinched at the words, revealing what Acton suspected. The senator knew damn well this could go south, yet had invited him regardless. "How about we leave our families out of this, Professor."

Acton's blood boiled. "You have the luxury of doing so, Senator, I do not. My family is here with me under the assurances that we would be perfectly safe." He jabbed a finger toward the helicopter. "I assume that's for you?"

"It is."

"And what about us?"

"My understanding is there's a second helicopter nearby, but there's not enough room for two of them to land here."

"Then talk to whoever is in charge here and have them bring in our chopper. We are leaving."

"Professor, you need to calm down."

Acton pressed a finger into the man's chest. "And you need to wake up. If you want to put your own life at risk just to make a statement to the Chinese, that's your right, but you dragged us along, and even if you thought it was safe at the time, it no longer is. Chinese troops are landing. You saw it, I saw it. They wouldn't do that if they weren't planning on invading. This place is a target, and we're all sitting ducks the moment

129

you leave in your chopper. Don't you think they've got people positioned in the area watching for you to leave? The moment you're clear, they're going to radio in the airstrike that takes out this facility, and we're all still here. It's time to take responsibility, Senator, and show us whether you actually have the balls you pretend to have on TV. Let the people you're responsible for leave on your chopper and you take ours."

"Is there a problem here?"

Acton turned to see Bradley approaching rapidly. Acton removed the finger still pressed into Simmons' chest as the senator shook his head. "No, Rick, no problem. Professor Acton was just reminding me of my responsibility for my guests' safety."

Bradley addressed Acton. "I can assure you, sir, you're perfectly safe here."

Acton glared at him. "Don't feed me the party line. You and I both know that's bullshit. The Chinese are landing troops behind the front lines. There's only one reason to do that. They intend to invade. For the love of God, learn from your history. We did the same thing on D-Day. It's been done countless times. The only reason they aren't bombing the shit out of this place right now is because the senator is here. You and I both know the moment he leaves in that chopper, everyone here is dead." He turned to Simmons. "So, Senator, I'll ask you again, why don't you let the people you're responsible for leave in your chopper and you take ours?"

Simmons opened his mouth to respond but Bradley cut him off. "Out of the question, Professor. I'll remind you of the waivers you signed before joining the senator. While every attempt will be made to protect you and your people, security's main priority is the senator. That chopper has certain capabilities that the one allotted to you doesn't, capabilities that are required should we be in a state of war."

"Then swap them. The senator assures me our chopper is nearby."

"It is, however, it would take several minutes to exchange positions, and in that time, the senator would be vulnerable."

"Why would he be vulnerable? Everyone keeps telling me that as long as his ass is sitting on this piece of real estate, we're all perfectly safe."

"You are, Professor, however, I have to plan for the worst-case scenario." Bradley extended an arm, placing it between Simmons and Acton. "Senator, they're waiting for you inside."

Simmons nodded. "I'll be there in a moment, Rick."

"Very well, sir." Bradley stepped away, though not out of sight.

Simmons closed the gap, slightly lowering his voice. "Listen, Professor, I truly am sorry about this, and please don't take this the wrong way, but if it were just you and your wife, there would be room on the chopper. You changed the plans by bringing your friends. There just isn't room for five of you. I was assured that wouldn't be a problem because there'd be a second chopper available. Bradley is too good a man to say it, but our hosts reassigned one of the chopper pads to parking to make room for additional local dignitaries. There was always supposed to be two choppers here. I would happily take the risk and have the choppers swapped out, but when it comes to security, even I don't have a say. It prevents people from guilting us politicians into doing things that might risk our lives by leaving such matters in the hands of our security team who have orders to ignore anything we request. It stops us from allowing our emotions to get in the way of our personal safety."

While Acton believed the man, he ignored most of what was said as he focused on what the senator undoubtedly thought was a trivial fact. "You said if there were just two of us, there'd be room on your chopper."

"Yes, but there's five of you."

"I'm aware of that, but you still have those two seats."

Simmons' eyes widened slightly. "Yes, if you and your wife want them, they're yours."

Acton wanted to smack the man for the very suggestion he or Laura would take one of the seats over the others. "I want you to let Tommy and Mai go with you."

Simmons' jaw dropped for a brief moment then snapped shut. "Of course. I'm sorry, Professor, I never meant to suggest you were trying to save yourself. Your two young friends are absolutely welcome on the chopper—" He caught himself and beckoned Bradley over.

The man jogged up to them. "Yes, Senator?"

"Those two seats originally meant for the professors. They're still available?"

"Yes, sir."

"Then the two young adults, Tommy and Mai, will be taking those two seats."

"Understood, sir."

Simmons tapped Bradley's chest with his index finger. "We don't leave until they're on the chopper."

Bradley opened his mouth to protest but instead nodded curtly. "Understood, Senator." He walked away and joined the other security team members, leaving Acton to wonder if the man was merely humoring the senator or if he truly meant it.

Simmons extended a hand and Acton took it. "I'm genuinely sorry for the situation I've put you and your loved ones in. This was supposed to be a harmless visit. Show the flag then have a pleasant excursion to see a local curiosity shared with some of my constituents. I never would have agreed to bring you along if I had known what was going to happen."

Acton's eyes narrowed. "Agreed to take us along? My understanding is you do this all the time."

"I do." He paused. "I'm sorry, I thought you knew. I didn't choose you. You were chosen for me."

Acton's chest tightened. "What do you mean, I was chosen for you? You mean someone in your office picked me from a list?" Yet he already knew the answer to that question before Simmons shook his head.

"No. I have half a dozen archaeologists that I normally use that have been vetted, and I've come to know over the years. Frankly, Professor, I had never heard of you until a couple of days ago."

"Then who?"

"I'm not at liberty to say. All I will say, Professor, is that after seeing you in action today during that cave-in, I know exactly why you were recommended."

"And why is that?

"Because, Professor, in the heat of the moment, you took action. You assessed the situation and took command immediately before even my own people reacted. You remained calm the entire time and saved all our lives. I read your file, and I haven't seen a civilian's that heavily redacted in years. You're more than what your faculty page on your university's website says, so ask yourself, Professor, why are you here?"

Acton unclenched his fists. "I'm here because whoever recommended me knew this was going to happen."

"Exactly. Someone was coming, Professor, and I know the people that I normally bring, and while experts in their field and brilliant men and women, I couldn't imagine any of them acting with a level head like I've seen you do so far. You're here to save lives, and your level-headedness not only already saved all the lives from that cave, but you just saved your two young friends by seeing past your anger and through my short-sightedness, and ensuring them passage on my helicopter. Now all you need to do is continue to think straight, and I have no doubt the three of you will safely survive whatever happens today." Simmons patted him on the arm. "Good luck, Professor, and I'll see you on the other side." He turned and entered the facility with Bradley, and Acton found himself surrounded by Laura, Reading, Tommy, and Mai.

"What did he say?" asked Laura. "You seemed quite upset."

"Yeah, I thought you were going to deck him," said Tommy.

Acton held up a hand, cutting off the questions so he could answer them. "No time to get into all the details, but basically, we're on our own. Our chopper won't be brought in until after the senator's leaves. There's no way for us to take the senator's chopper and him take ours, and there's no way for them to swap the helicopters."

"Bloody hell!" Reading glared in the direction the senator had disappeared. "They have to have known that would put us at risk."

"It's not entirely their fault. Apparently, the Indians repurposed one of the helipads as parking for the event. Also, there were only supposed to be two of us, and we would have fit in the senator's chopper." Acton looked at Tommy and Mai. "So, the good news is that those two seats are still available on the senator's helicopter, and you two are taking them."

Mai stared at him, aghast. "You mean, leave without you?"

"Yes. We're all safe until the senator's chopper lifts off. You two are going to be on it, which means you'll be safe no matter what happens."

"But what about you?" asked Tommy. "This isn't fair."

Acton placed a hand on Tommy's shoulder. "You two are our responsibility, which means you two are getting on the chopper." He turned to Laura. "Agreed?"

"Of course."

He looked at Reading.

"You have to ask?"

Acton smiled. "No, I suppose not. So, the senator's security guy Bradley knows the deal, as does the senator. I want the two of you to go inside, get changed into your formal wear, and stay glued to Bradley."

"Shouldn't we stick to the senator?" asked Mai.

Acton shook his head. "I doubt you'll be able to. Remember, he's a dignitary who will be pressing flesh and giving a speech. Bradley will be hanging back on the periphery. Stick near him, then make sure you get on that helicopter."

Tommy's eyes narrowed. "Why do we need to get in our formal wear? Is that really important in the middle of a crisis?"

"If you're dressed up, there's no doubt you're a guest, but if you're dressed like you are now, somebody's liable to think you're the help and not let you go someplace you need to. If the Indians think you're a dignitary and something goes wrong, they'll do whatever they can to protect you. So, I want the two of you to go in there now, get changed, stick to Bradley, and get on that chopper. When you get to New Delhi, go to the hotel. Hopefully, by the time you get there, there'll be a message from us. If there isn't, call Greg, let him know what's happened, and he'll know what to do."

Mai burst into tears and thrust into Laura's arms. Tommy's head dropped into his chest, a loud sniff belying his struggle to control his own emotions. Acton put his arm over the young man's shoulders and gave him a squeeze.

"It's going to be all right. You two will be safe, and that's the most important thing. But you have to go in now, play your part, and take care of yourselves. We're going to be leaving, which means we won't be here to help you if something goes wrong. Stick with Bradley."

Laura let go of Mai and Reading handed her a handkerchief. She dried her eyes, whispering a thank you.

"Now go, just in case they decide to wise up and end this ceremony. You need to get changed and find Bradley right away."

Mai hugged him hard. "Please be careful."

Acton hugged her back. "Don't worry, we'll be fine. We've been in worse situations than this before, and this time we've got Hugh with us, and he's too damn stubborn to die." He gently pushed her away and toward the door. "Off you go now. We'll see you in New Delhi."

They reluctantly climbed the steps then disappeared through the doors, but not before giving one final tear-filled wave. Laura fell into his arms as he struggled to contain his own emotions, his stomach in knots, his chest aching.

Laura sniffed. "My God, this must be what it feels like when a kid leaves for college."

"More like war." Reading sighed. "They'll be fine, so for now, we push them out of our minds and selfishly worry about our own asses. What's our plan?"

"While I'm open to suggestions, I'm thinking we get in that SUV we arrived in, and head west as fast as we can, just like Major Singh suggested in the first place. Whatever is happening here is happening soon. The risk to us isn't here"—he stabbed a finger toward the road—"it's out there. We don't know where those Chinese Special Forces are, so we want to be past their line when they hit this place."

Reading agreed. "Their orders are probably to take out the defensive systems, then any targets of opportunity."

Laura shivered. "Targets of opportunity. What a horrible way to think of ourselves."

Acton surveyed the area. "Did anybody see our driver?"

Reading indicated a side entrance. "He went through that door over there."

"Okay, I'm going to go find him. You two go find our luggage. Grab anything you think is useful, especially that satellite phone. We'll meet right back here. I want to be leaving this rock in less than ten minutes."

Reading grunted. "Let's try to make it five. I have a bad feeling about this entire situation."

Over the Arabian Sea

Less than half an hour ago, somebody in Beijing had started throwing shit at a fan. Dawson and his team had been activated and now sat in the back of a V-22 Osprey, barreling across the Arabian Sea and into Indian territory for insertion into the conflict zone the Chinese were expected to be crawling over within the next two hours. Their commanding officer, Colonel Clancy, said the Indians had approved the over-flight though hadn't given permission to land, which was fine by Dawson— they hadn't asked for permission, and time was of the essence here.

Ideally, the senator and his people, including the professors, would have safely made it out of the area by the time his team arrived, and they would be redeployed elsewhere if necessary or would return to the carrier strike group. But if their targets hadn't made it to safety, an insertion was in order.

Niner leaned forward. "So, BD, are we going in Kung Fu fighting, or are we just supposed to hug any Chinese we find?"

Dawson wagged his tablet. "They haven't finalized the ROEs yet. Right now, we don't even have clearance to insert."

Atlas cursed. "And what happens if we arrive there and we still don't have clearance?"

"If we don't have clearance, then I'm sure it's because either everyone's safe or the Chinese have backed down."

"But they're landing paratroopers behind the lines."

Spock shook his head. "There's no way they're just dropping in to say hello and pick up some butter chicken with a side of naan."

Dawson agreed. "I have no doubt things are heading south fast. Washington is just hedging their bets. They don't want anything on the record that has the US military getting involved before hostilities begin."

Niner leaned back. "So, this ceremony the docs are attending is formal?"

Spock cocked an eyebrow. "Why the hell would that matter?"

Niner shrugged. "I just wonder what Laura will be wearing."

"You have a girlfriend!" shouted the team.

Niner flinched. "I'm really not good at this boyfriend thing, am I?"

Jagger leaned forward and patted Niner's knee. "Don't worry about it. Practice makes perfect, and the way you're going, Angela will probably dump you before the end of the month and you can try again in four or five years."

Niner sighed. "I don't know. Things are going really well. Who knows? She could be the one."

Atlas closed his eyes. "So, what you're saying is you've already picked out your wedding dress."

Snickers filled the cabin and Dawson's chest tightened with the mention of wedding dresses. The tragedy that had befallen the Unit only weeks ago began after an afternoon of shopping for dresses for his impending nuptials. Maggie was still recovering, the wedding plans placed on hold yet again. He understood why. They seemed cursed. Every time it appeared fate would give them a chance to move forward, something happened that killed those dreams.

"Hey, BD, you with us?"

He snapped back to reality to see Atlas waving a hand in his face. "Sorry, got lost in thought there." He finally noticed that everyone was staring out the windows. "What's going on?"

"See for yourself." Atlas jerked his chin toward the window behind Dawson. He turned and peered out.

"What am I looking—" He cut himself off at the sight of two Indian Air Force Sukhoi Su-30MKI fighter jets taking up position on their wing.

Niner pressed against the window beside him. "I wonder if they're here to escort us to where we want to go, or where they want us to go?"

A voice crackled over the speakers. "Sergeant Major, please join me in the cockpit."

"I guess we're about to find out."

Indian Army Northern Command Communications Center
Uttarakhand, India

Acton spotted Veer chatting excitedly with several others dressed similarly to him, no doubt sharing what he had seen in the skies on his way here, if the fear on their faces were any indication. Veer noticed him approaching and hissed, cutting off the conversation. Everyone turned to face Acton as he walked up and Veer bowed. "Sir, are you lost? The reception is through the other entrance."

Acton shook his head. "No. We're leaving immediately."

"But the ceremony hasn't begun."

Acton leaned in, lowering his voice, and had to suppress a smile at the almost comic display of everyone else he didn't want to hear what he was about to say, leaning in as well. "You know as well as I do that the moment the senator's chopper leaves the pad, this place becomes a target. I intend to be gone long before that happens."

"But don't you have a helicopter waiting for you?"

"Yes, but it's not here. It could take five or ten minutes before it gets here, and that could be too late. We're leaving now. You can come with us, or just give me the keys."

Veer recoiled in horror at the idea. "Oh, I can't give you the keys! I signed out that vehicle. It's my responsibility."

Acton clenched his fists then released the grip. They didn't have time for this. "Ask yourself this. When you're dead and the vehicle is destroyed by the missile attack that's going to happen within five minutes of the senator leaving, who fills out the paperwork?"

Veer stared at him blankly for a moment. "I see your point. Meet me out front in ten minutes. I need to make sure we're fully fueled up, and get some supplies for the trip."

"Skip the supplies and make it five."

Veer quickly headed deeper into the complex. Acton spotted a bathroom and made a beeline for it, uncertain when he'd get another chance, and as he entered, he paused, a round of applause audible in the background. He checked his watch. 45 minutes early. He continued inside as he wondered who had changed the schedule. Was it the senator's people, or the Indians? There had barely been enough time for the man to change into his formal attire, and he just hoped Tommy and Mai weren't left behind should the advanced ceremony turn into an abbreviated one as well.

As he did his business, something gnawed at him. He had been specifically recommended to accompany the senator. It meant somebody had intentionally put him and his loved ones in danger. And when this was all over, he wanted to know who the hell that was.

A klaxon sounded and he quickly zipped up then sprinted toward the exit, not bothering to confirm what it meant. He burst through the doors into the cool afternoon air and spotted Reading and Laura running down the steps from the main entrance. He hailed them as he rushed toward them. "Did you get everything?"

They both held up bags.

"Good. Our driver is supposed to be topping up the car."

"How much time do you think we have?" asked Laura.

"It can't be more than a few minutes."

The first of the guests inside shoved through the doors, signaling the beginning of chaos. Laura stared at the jammed parking lot then at the road leading to the gate. "Can we get far enough away on foot?"

Reading shook his head. "I can't, but you two might be able to." He quickly embraced them, giving each a brief hug, then pushed them away, pointing at the road leading away from the complex. "Go now. Don't waste a moment. I'll try to get us a vehicle and pick you up."

"Bullshit to that!" exclaimed Acton. "If you think for a second—"

"Look!" Laura pointed behind him.

Acton spun and watched the senator's chopper lift off from the roof. Laura hugged him as it gained altitude then banked away from the facility. "Thank God, Tommy and Mai are safe."

Reading pushed the two of them away. "And now it's time for you two to get safe. That's an order. Don't let your stubbornness get you killed. You sacrificed your seats to save them. Let me sacrifice myself to save you. Now go."

Acton stared his friend in the eyes for a moment, unable to find the words that would convey how he felt about him and what he was doing. Laura sobbed beside him, falling into Reading's arms. Reading reached out and squeezed Acton's shoulder.

"Tell Spencer I love him."

Acton gripped his friend's hand. "You can count on it." He pointed at the parking lot. "Steal a car if you have to. I expect to see you soon." He grabbed Laura and they sprinted down the road toward the gate, his heart aching as his wife continued to cry. He came to a stop. "I can't do this."

Laura grabbed him, burying her head in his chest. "Neither can I."

They turned back toward the compound, Simmons' chopper with Tommy and Mai still visible to the west. "At least the kids are safe."

The helicopter suddenly tipped forward into a nosedive then a fireball erupted. Laura screamed as it was erased from existence.

Along with Tommy and Mai.

Northwest of the Indian Army Northern Command Communications Center

Uttarakhand, India

Captain Kumar peered through the scope of his SIG Sauer SIG716i rifle. The mobile SAM battery was within sight, set up in a clearing just off the road that cut through the valley. Camouflage netting concealed it from the distant observer, but the Chinese had evidently already determined its location since they had a Special Forces team on the ground ready to take it out. According to his briefing before deployment, the hardened installations didn't appear to be targeted by ground forces, only the mobile. That suggested the Chinese intended to use missiles to take out the permanent defenses his country had deployed.

But that wasn't his concern. His mission was to protect this particular mobile site if the Chinese were indeed going to invade. Their superior air power would be critical in the opening hours and days. They would launch cruise missiles from across the border, taking out the permanent defenses they had already located. There was nothing his side could do about that. These mobile sites were critical, which was why the Chinese had been inserting troops over the past several days. If his country could keep enough of these sites online, when the Chinese did send fighters across, installations like this could take out dozens of their aircraft if given the opportunity. But if his team and the others like them, spread throughout the region, were to fail, this entire area could rapidly fall.

He checked his watch. The ceremony wasn't supposed to start for another half hour, and his latest update was that the festivities after the fact were being cut short. The moment the senator lifted off in his chopper, they expected the Chinese to act. The ground teams would likely be first, taking out the mobile units before missiles would launch against the fixed installations. Planes would cross the border to take out other hard targets, perhaps dropping paratroopers in large numbers, and open up the way for ground forces to pour across the border and into the nation he had vowed to protect.

It couldn't be allowed.

His comms squawked in his ear. "Zero-One, Zero-Six. I've got activity from my location. It looks like they're moving in, over."

Kumar scanned the area with his scope, confirming the six Chinese soldiers in his sights were still holding their positions. "Zero-Six, Zero-One. Negative activity at this location." One of the Chinese moved in his scope and he cursed as everyone now advanced, scurrying from rock to rock. "Correction, we now have activity here. Stand by." He switched frequencies. "Control, this is Whiskey-Zulu Zero-One. We have activity at our location. It appears the Chinese are moving early. What are our orders?"

"Stand by, Zero-One."

There was a click and a new voice filled his ear. It was Colonel Mandal, his CO. "Zero-One, Control Actual. Confirm they're not just repositioning."

"Impossible to say for certain, Control, however, if they reposition any closer, they'll be able to stir the rice our men are cooking."

There was a pause before the order came. "Control Actual to all teams, take out your targets."

A string of acknowledgments responded, including Kumar's. He switched frequencies. "This is Zero-One. Execute in three...two...one...execute."

Gunfire erupted all around him and from two other positions surrounding the SAM site. He eliminated his two targets within his arc and scanned left to see two more down. The weapon to his right fell silent as he leaned left, confirming through his scope that all six hostiles were down. Gunfire continued from Team Two's position at his 10 o'clock as he indicated for his men to advance.

"Team Two, report," he whispered as they moved forward.

"Weapons misfire. Two targets managed to take cover and are returning fire. Stand by."

He continued forward, covering his men as they checked to confirm their targets were permanently neutralized. "Team Three, report."

"Team Three secure," was the immediate reply.

"Copy that, Team Three. Confirm your kills then move to assist Team Two."

"Roger that. Kills already confirmed. Repositioning now."

Kumar took up position behind a rock then peered out using his scope to assess the situation. Gunfire continued to rattle from Team Two's position. The SAM site was still secure, its defensive group, not given prior warning as to their situation and what was being done about it, uncertain as to what was going on. He rose, signaling the advance on the remaining Chinese, when one of his men grunted and collapsed where he stood, the thunderclap of a sniper rifle echoing in the valley a moment later.

"Take cover! We've got a sniper!"

But the warning came too late for another of his men who dropped, a red mist erupting from his chest. As the report of the sniper rifle filled his ears once again, he noted the position of his man's wound, then dove behind a large rock, putting it between him and where he suspected the sniper was positioned.

Behind them.

"This is Zero-One. Sniper is behind our position to the south. Make sure you're behind north-facing cover."

Another shot rang out, the bullet ricocheting off the stone to his right.

"Raj, are you all right?" he shouted to the one remaining man on his team.

"I'm good. We're pinned down here unless we can find this guy."

A .50 caliber abruptly opened up. Kumar flattened himself against the ground before realizing whoever was firing wasn't aiming at his position. Raj figured it out at the same time.

"It's coming from the SAM battery!"

149

Kumar smiled. "Excellent. While they've got him distracted, let's see if we can spot the bastard." He turned around and took a knee, readying his weapon. He leaned out slightly and noted where the .50 cal gunner was aiming. He seemed focused on one area, which suggested he had spotted something—if he hadn't, he would be spraying the entire area with suppression fire.

Kumar peered through his scope, quickly scanning the area, but spotted nothing. He took a deep breath and held it, steadying his nerves, then checked again, this time slowly, methodically passing his eye over every stone, every rock, every outcropping. It was a futile effort. If the target were hiding behind a rock, he could pass over him a dozen times and never know he was there.

Another thunderclap and the .50 fell silent.

"Do you see him?" he shouted to Raj.

"No, I've got nothing!"

Kumar glanced over his shoulder to see the body of the brave soldier who had been manning the heavy machine gun pulled to the ground, another taking his place, the weapon belching lead once again.

We're never going to get him like this.

"Zero-Six, Zero-One. What's your status, over?"

"Zero-One, Zero-Six, we're secure."

"Copy that. Watch your sixes, but reposition left and right of our original position and advance on that sniper. We need to take him out."

"Roger that. Repositioning now."

Another shot from the sniper rifle rang out and the faint cry of a soldier at the SAM site had Kumar shaking his head. He activated his comms. "This is Zero-One. Concentrate your focus left and right of where the fifty is firing. I don't think our sniper is where the gunner thinks he is."

"Got him!" shouted Raj from his left.

"Where?"

"Left of where they're currently firing. Thirty meters. There's a large rock with a sheer black face and two medium-sized to its left."

Kumar slowly leaned to his right, the scope swinging fast in the opposite direction, revealing the rocks in question. "Got it."

"Ten meters below. He's behind a medium-sized white stone. You can't miss it, it's the only one there."

Kumar lifted his shoulder, his scope filled with gray rocks until finally he spotted the white one in question, slightly to the left. He focused in on it. "I don't see him. Do you?"

"No, he's taking cover right now. Probably reloading."

"All right. Hold your fire until you have a clear shot. I don't want him to know we're on to him."

"Copy that."

Kumar readied himself. The Chinese sniper was far enough away that it was approaching the maximum range for his weapon, but he was still within it. The shot would have to be a good one. He steadied his breathing as he focused on the task at hand. "What side of the rock did you last see him on?"

"Our left, always our left."

"Copy that." It meant a right-handed sniper. He adjusted again.

"Here he comes!"

"Take the shot if you have it," ordered Kumar as their target leaned into sight.

"Taking the shot."

Kumar squeezed the trigger simultaneously and smiled as the target jerked back, collapsing on the rocks, unmoving. "This is Zero-One. Target neutralized. Team Two, secure him and sweep the area. Team Three, get that SAM ready to move. I have no doubt the Chinese have radioed in its position."

A string of acknowledgments came back and he turned, waving at the .50 cal gunner to hold their fire. The weapon fell silent and Kumar rose, slowly assessing the situation, searching for any sign there were further hostiles. Finding none, he walked toward the SAM site, Raj joining him. Team Three was already there, the grateful soldiers they had just helped save shaking hands and exchanging hugs before scrambling to ready the weapon for repositioning.

He heard something behind him that sent his heart hammering and he spun. "Everyone take cover!" he shouted as he sprinted away from the weapon system, damning to hell the Chinese bastard who had launched the missile about to kill everyone.

Operations Center 2, CIA Headquarters

Langley, Virginia

Leroux stared at the screen in stunned silence, the satellite footage showing the helicopter's wreckage with its full load of fuel now a raging cauldron of death. His stomach churned with the implications.

"Tommy," whispered Tong, her voice cracking.

They had both worked with him several times in the past couple of years. He was a good kid, brilliant, and full of life. And now in an instant, if the last update from Simmons' team was accurate, he and his girlfriend were gone. Leroux drew a deep breath, forcing himself back into the moment. There was a job to do, and what had just happened could lead to all-out war. He glanced over his shoulder at Marc Therrien, one of their best at analyzing footage for anomalies. "Check every satellite image we have of that area. I want to know what took down that chopper. Was it a missile or a bomb?"

"I'm on it."

"Holy shit!" exclaimed Child.

Leroux turned. "What?"

Child pointed at the main screen. Leroux spun to see the tactical display now showing dozens of missiles, some still heading toward the border, others already crossing it. He cursed then pointed at Tong. "Notify the Chief that this is going down." He turned to Therrien. "Notify our asset on the ground."

"Yes, sir."

He turned to Child. "Get me footage of that facility. And somebody track those missiles. Are any of them heading for the primary target?"

Tong hung up her phone. "The Chief is on his way. I'm on the missile tracking."

Therrien shouted from the back of the room. "Our ground asset has acknowledged."

Leroux gave him a thumbs-up as he turned his attention to the displays. "Sonya, what have you got for me?"

Tong hammered at her keyboard. "I've got nine missiles that could possibly target the facility. I've colored them orange."

Leroux's eyes shifted to the tactical display, the missiles in question changing from red to orange, the primary target highlighted with a pulsing green indicator. "Time to first impact?"

"Three minutes."

Leroux cursed. There was no way in hell anyone was getting out of there alive. His eyes narrowed. "What's happening?"

Tong reexamined her terminal. "All nine are still inbound, but three appear to be heading to different targets. Six still likely to hit the complex."

The door hissed open and Morrison rushed in, his eyes instantly glued to the displays. "Survivors?"

Leroux shook his head. "No evidence of any."

"Nobody is surviving that," muttered Child.

Morrison joined Leroux at the center of the room. "Any word from our asset?"

"Only acknowledgment of the incoming missiles."

"Get him."

Tong gently spoke into her mic then shook her head. "I can't make contact." She held up a finger as she pressed the headphone against her ear.

Morrison stared at her. "Well?"

"It's him."

"What did he say?"

She smiled. "He said, 'Wait an effing minute. I'm busy trying not to die here.'"

Indian Army Northern Command Communications Center

Uttarakhand, India

Ten Minutes Earlier

Jack—just Jack—spotted the senator and his team enter the room, Simmons appearing spiffy in his suit, the transformation from dorky adult Boy Scout to seasoned professional politician, impressive. If the senator was here, that meant so were the professors and the others. An announcement had been made only moments ago that they had pushed up the official ribbon-cutting by almost 45 minutes, which meant the Indians were nervous. The thinking the entire time, whether in Washington or New Delhi, was that everyone was safe as long as the senator was on the premises.

But something had changed.

He headed toward a side door several of the security staff had used since he arrived. With credentials that had him as part of the press, he made for the door and opened it, stepping through as if he owned the place. He flashed his ID to a startled soldier, no doubt assigned to make sure guests weren't searching for a bathroom through the wrong door.

"I need to speak to whoever is in charge of security, immediately."

The soldier snapped to attention and pointed at a man at the far end of the hall. "Colonel Khan is in charge."

"Thank you." Jack strode swiftly toward the man in a heated discussion with someone on the other end of the phone pressed to his ear. The colonel didn't appear pleased. Jack presented his Langley-forged credentials and the colonel held up a finger, continuing the conversation in Hindi as applause broke out behind them, the ceremony evidently beginning.

Colonel Khan finally ended his call. "Guests aren't supposed to be in this area."

"I'm not a guest, Colonel. I'm a member of the senator's security detail." He again flashed his identification. "I need to know why you moved up the ceremony."

The colonel grabbed the ID and scrutinized it, his eyes narrowing. "You aren't a member of the senator's detail. You're listed as a member of the press."

"Colonel, I'm whoever I need to be in order to protect those I'm responsible for."

Khan regarded him for a moment before his eyebrows rose. "I see. Well, Mr. White, I don't have time to deal with the CIA or the NSA or whoever the hell you claim to be working for. For all I know, you could be working for the Chinese. I'm afraid I have to treat you as yet another infiltrator."

Jack held out a hand, cutting off the colonel. "Another? You mean someone's infiltrated the complex?"

Khan eyed him then finally cursed. "I'm going to take a chance that you're telling the truth. Ten minutes ago, we caught one of our people near the senator's helicopter. He wasn't authorized for that area, then when we checked him against our database, we found out he was an imposter."

"Chinese?"

"He certainly doesn't appear Chinese, but he could be working for them. He's being questioned right now. I've had his picture and prints sent to Northern Command Headquarters for identification."

Jack cursed. "You obviously have a problem. And who's to say he's the only one? Have you swept the helicopter?"

"We're in the process now."

Jack growled. "We don't have time for this shit. We need to end this ceremony right now and get these people out of here."

"You won't get any argument from me, Mr. White. However, the senator and my commanding officer strongly disagree."

"You mean the senator knows about this?"

"Yes. And to quote the man directly, he said, 'The longer I speak, the more thoroughly you can search the helicopter for any tampering. And I'm not about to let the Chinese cut short my speech.'"

Jack groaned. "That sounds like Simmons, all right. All balls, no brains." He shook his head. "I can't believe his security chief would accept that."

"He wasn't there. I don't think he knows."

Jack cursed. "How long do your men need to check that chopper?"

"Hours? Days? We don't know if anything was done to it. My men swear they caught him approaching the helicopter, but they might be covering their asses. An explosive could have been placed on board or something could have been tampered with so that it falls out of the sky. And the problem with something like that is, how long do you search without finding anything before you give up? In one hour, the senator is scheduled to leave, and at best, we'd be able to sweep it for explosives. And in the meantime, we might have another infiltrator planting the bomb that his partner failed to do. We could be playing into their hands by giving more people access. It might have been the plan all along."

A thought occurred to Jack that had a pit forming in his stomach. "Or a bomb was planted at the ceremony. That's far more likely than getting something on the chopper."

Khan's eyes bulged. "We need to clear that room, but how? He'll never agree to stop his speech."

"There's only one thing we can do."

"What's that?"

"Make it impossible for the senator to give his speech."

Tommy stumbled through the bathroom door, sporting his best suit. He could count on one hand, perhaps two, how many times he had worn one. And he couldn't stand it. He stared down at his tie, straightening it for the umpteenth time, when someone cleared their throat. He looked up to see Mai standing in front of him in her figure-hugging pants suit. "Wow!" he gasped.

She smiled. "You think?"

"Oh yeah, I think."

She held out her hand and he took it. "Let's go, we don't have time to waste on you gawking at me. We need to find Bradley."

Tommy followed her down the corridor, though not before letting her get ahead of him by a couple of paces so he could check her out. Mai glanced back at him, catching him in the act. "Are you staring at my ass?"

He grinned. "Who? Me?"

"We might be about to go to war. Start thinking with the other head."

In the rush, he had forgotten what was happening, the reason they were here in this moment. The professors had sacrificed their own lives to save them, and in his determination to focus on the task at hand of making himself appear presentable for the reception, he had been disrespectful. He murmured an apology and she ignored it as a guard with a smile held open a door just ahead. They stepped through to find the senator at the front of the room, surrounded by various dignitaries with a crowd of perhaps thirty or forty in front of them wearing a mix of uniforms, suits, and dresses.

Mai pointed to their left. "There he is."

Tommy turned in the direction she was pointing and spotted Bradley, the man's head on a swivel. He noticed them and pointed at the floor beside him, indicating where he wanted them. Tommy breathed a sigh of relief as they scurried around the edge of the crowd to join the man evidently sticking to the agreement.

Suddenly an alarm sounded, silencing whoever was speaking. Bradley rushed forward toward the senator, followed by two other members of the detail. Before anyone else in the room had time to react, Bradley already had his charge heading toward an exit. The sight of the senator being hurried away, combined with the wailing siren, triggered a panic, and everyone in the room rushed toward the main entrance.

Simmons and his team disappeared through a door and Tommy cursed. He grabbed Mai and sprinted toward it, pushing their way through the panicked guests. He lunged forward and grabbed the handle just before the pneumatic door closer completed its job. He hauled it open and thrust Mai through then followed.

"There!" gasped Mai, pointing at the far end of the corridor, Simmons and the others disappearing from sight. They rushed down the hall, Mai's heels clicking on the concrete, and he glanced down at the impractical shoes.

"Why did you wear those?"

She glared at him. "I'm supposed to wear hiking boots? We were never supposed to be running, remember?"

She was right. At the end of the ceremony, they were supposed to board a chopper and leave in an orderly fashion. But at the moment, the deal brokered between Acton and the senator appeared to have been thrown out the window with the sounding of the alarm. They continued down the corridor as quickly as Mai's shoes would allow. A door at the far end closed, the only indicator of where the senator and his people had gone. Tommy sprinted ahead and pulled on the handle. "It's locked!" he cried, hammering on the door.

The door was suddenly thrown open, knocking him off his feet. He stumbled backward and slammed into the wall opposite. Mai reached him as someone stepped through the door, the pounding of footfalls in what was apparently a stairwell on the other side continuing past. Tommy regained his footing and finally looked up to see who had burst through the door, and cried out in relief.

It was Jack.

"We can't go, not without the kids!"

Bradley ignored Simmons' protests, instead ordering the chopper pilot to lift off. Simmons stared back at the door they had come through, praying for it to open, for the young man and woman whom he had sworn to protect to appear. But as the helicopter rose then banked away from the pad, he slumped back in his seat and closed his eyes. When he had served in the military, the doctrine of No Man Left Behind was drummed into them, and he had already failed with the professors and their Interpol friend. In his defense, they had already taken matters into their own hands and were planning on leaving before the end of the ceremony, and long before the Chinese were expected to strike.

But for some reason an alarm had sounded, perhaps signaling an airstrike was imminent, and condemning those he was responsible for. He said another prayer for their souls and all left behind, but the guilt that racked him was reserved for young Tommy and Mai. They were merely in the springtime of their lives, now condemned to death because his security chief had followed protocol and ignored anything his charge had said where it might compromise his safety—including the agreement to take responsibility for the safety of the young guests. There was no point arguing it now—Bradley was too good at his job.

He opened his mouth to ask what could be done but Bradley was already on his comms.

"ETA on that second chopper?" Bradley cursed, apparently not pleased with the reply. "What do you mean fifteen minutes? It should have been scrambled the moment that alarm sounded! And we were assured it was only five minutes away regardless!" There was another pause and he cursed again. "Then get the damn thing here as soon as you can...wait a minute, repeat that." His face reddened and his eyes shot wide. "He said what?" His head spun as he apparently searched for something.

"What is it?" asked Simmons, fear setting in.

"They're saying an infiltrator might have placed a bomb on the chopper!"

Everyone began searching and Simmons' heart went into overdrive as he joined the hunt.

"Get us on the ground, now!" shouted Bradley, and the pilot shoved forward on the stick, sending them into a nosedive as the frantic search continued. And then, without warning, the gates of Hell opened upon them, and after a moment of suffering, Senator Simmons' guilt was ended as he was delivered for justice in a court far more final than any in this realm.

A rumble in the distance had them all cocking an ear. "What was that?" asked Mai.

Jack couldn't be certain, but he had a pretty damned good idea. "I think that might have been your ride."

Tommy's jaw dropped. "What do you mean? Our helicopter with the senator?"

Jack grabbed Mai by the hand, knowing Tommy would follow, and sprinted toward the opposite end of the corridor then cursed at the clicking of her heels and the constant tug on his arm. He stopped, turned around, and grabbed her, lifting her over his shoulder into a fireman's carry. He spun around and continued toward the door at the far end at a much brisker pace, Tommy on his heels. Mai didn't protest and Jack thanked God she was a tiny little thing.

"Where are you taking us?" she cried. "Shouldn't we be getting to the other helicopter?"

Jack reached out for the door handle just ahead. "It won't be here in time. We have missiles incoming now."

"Holy shit!" Tommy sprinted ahead of them and yanked open the door.

Jack carried Mai outside then put her down as he continued toward an SUV parked at the side of the building, pre-positioned by him as his own personal escape route. He pulled the fob out of his pocket and pressed the button to unlock the doors, the lights flashing. "Both of you get in the back!"

He jumped in the driver's seat and fired up the engine as Tommy and Mai piled into the second row, the door slamming shut. He put the vehicle in gear and hammered on the gas, sending them around a one-way perimeter road he couldn't risk going the wrong way on as it was too narrow to get around an oncoming vehicle. The route delayed them but sent them around to the front of the building.

Which proved fortunate.

"There's Hugh!" cried Tommy, pointing ahead.

Jack hit the brakes, bringing them to a shuddering halt beside the Interpol agent. Jack rolled the passenger window down. "Get in!"

Reading stared blankly at him for a moment before his eyes shot wide and his hand darted out, yanking open the door. He climbed in and slammed it shut. Jack shoved the accelerator into the floor as Reading pointed ahead.

"Jim and Laura are just up ahead! Let's go! Let's go!"

Jack guided them down the winding road toward the gate and honked his horn three times. The professors were on their knees hugging each other at the side of the road. "What the hell are they doing?"

Reading closed his eyes as he gripped the dash. "The helicopter blew up. Tommy and Mai are dead."

Mai leaped between the seats and grabbed hold of the aging detective who apparently hadn't had time to look in the back during his rush to get inside. "We're alive!"

A startled Reading at first flinched at being grabbed, but when he realized who it was, he cried out in joy and hugged the young woman as if she were his own daughter, and reached out with his other hand to grip Tommy's shoulder. "I can't believe it! What happened?"

Jack swatted Mai and Reading. "There'll be enough time for chit-chat later. Get your head out that window and get the professors on their feet."

Mai let go and retreated to her seat as an elated Reading leaned out his window. "Jim! Laura! They're alive! They're alive!"

Acton looked up first, then Laura. Reading jerked a thumb over his shoulder at the back seat. "They're with me! Get inside!"

Acton's eyes shot wide and he leaped to his feet, hauling Laura up beside him as Jack brought them to a halt. Tommy leaned over and shoved the door open. Laura climbed in and screamed in delight, throwing herself at their young friends as Acton climbed in after her, hauling the door shut and tumbling into the rear row. Jack floored it, rapidly closing the gap with the vehicle in front of him, ending the tirade of protesting horns behind him. The gates were open and the guards waved them through, leaving them on a road with the choice of two directions.

East or west.

Too many were heading east, likely back toward the nearest population center, but Jack cranked the wheel to the right, hurtling them west and away from the 200,000 Chinese troops that were no doubt about to roll across the border at any moment if they weren't already. He spotted something in his side mirror and crouched for a better look. "Oh shit!" He pressed on the gas as hard as he could at the sight of contrails rapidly approaching. "Everybody hold on! This could get ugly!"

Seatbelts were fastened as Laura climbed over Mai's seat and dropped in beside her husband. A moment later, a terrific flash bathed the entire area in an unnatural glow and a fireball erupted behind them as missile after missile slammed into the complex, wiping out the newly found communications capability of the Indian Army in this region, and the lives of all those unfortunate enough to be left behind.

A shockwave of dust and debris regurgitated from the complex, racing in all directions. "Roll up your window!" he yelled at Reading who yanked up on the button, the window slowly closing as the wave overtook them. Jack squinted into the dust, attempting to read the road ahead, then slammed on the brakes as they were buffeted from the rear end. It might have just been his imagination, but he could have sworn the rear tires left the road. They slammed back down on the pavement and Jack brought them to a halt as everyone ducked, the howling of the shockwave passing over them finally abating.

He turned on the windshield wipers then pulled back on the stalk, sending a spray of washer fluid over the dirt and dust, turning it into mud before it finally cleared. He triggered the rear wiper washers as well then took his foot off the brakes, slowly easing them forward as the dust settled. Rock was strewn everywhere, though nothing the SUV couldn't clear, and he gradually gained speed.

Acton twisted in his seat, peering out the rear window. "My God! It's gone!"

Jack glanced in his side mirror then cursed. Nothing but rubble remained behind.

"Do you think there are survivors?" asked Laura.

"I doubt it," replied Jack. "If there are any, they're deep inside the complex and they'll need heavy equipment to be rescued." He held up a finger, heading off what was coming next. "And nobody talk about going back there to try and help. There's nothing we can do, and the Chinese could be landing paratroopers here any minute to secure the area. We have to get as far west as we can before it's too late."

167

As if to punctuate his assessment of the situation, fighter jets screamed overhead, heading west. He leaned forward and peered up at the sky, cursing yet again.

"Whose are they?" asked Laura.

"Chinese."

The war had begun.

Operations Center 2, CIA Headquarters
Langley, Virginia

Leroux and the others stared once again at the screen in shock. The complex was leveled, the chance of survivors slim to none, certainly not where they expected the professors and Reading were located in the building. Morrison was the first to recover and he gently tapped Leroux's arm.

Leroux flinched. "Sorry, Chief. Randy, start assessing the damage to see if you can spot any survivors. Sonya, start checking the surrounding area for hostiles then have someone give us an update on the border. Marc, try to make contact with our ground asset, see if Jack made it out of there."

Therrien thrust his hand in the air, snapping his fingers. "You have to hear this!"

The speakers overhead crackled. "I repeat, I'm okay, and I have them. I have the professors, I have Agent Reading, and I have Tommy and Mai."

169

A roar erupted from the operations center, even Morrison throwing his arms in the air before giving Leroux a hug. Leroux smiled then jacked into the conversation. "This is Control Actual. What's your location?"

"If you've got eyes on the area, we're in a black SUV heading west. We're maybe a mile from the facility."

"I've got him!" shouted Tong, the excitement in her voice evident to everyone. The large display at the front of the room showing various feeds was replaced with a single live image zoomed in on the SUV.

Leroux stepped closer. "Rawhide, we've got you. What are your intentions, over?"

"To head as far west as we can without running into any uninvited guests. What's the status? I just saw some Chinese J-10s blast past us."

"Stand by, Rawhide. We'll get you that tactical update as soon as we can. In the meantime, continue west and we'll monitor your path ahead."

"Copy that, Control." Jack's voice became subdued. "I assume you're aware of what happened to the senator's helicopter?"

"We're aware."

"Is there any word yet on the identity of the infiltrator?"

Leroux exchanged a puzzled glance with Morrison. "Rawhide, repeat your last. Did you say there was an infiltrator?"

"Confirmed, Control. The Indians arrested an impostor on the helipad only minutes before the helicopter was taken out. An Indian colonel I spoke with believed there was a chance he might have planted a bomb or tampered with the chopper."

Morrison pulled out his phone and made a call. As he stepped away, Leroux overheard enough of the murmured conversation to know what it was about.

"Rawhide, we're looking into that now. We'll update you as soon as we know anything."

"Copy that, Control. Rawhide, out."

Morrison ended his call and stared at the screen showing the SUV rapidly heading west. "Bring up the tactical display."

Tong tapped a few keys and the lone satellite image was replaced with a feed from the Pentagon, triggering a collective gasp that filled the room. Thousands of targets were in motion, icons indicating fighter jets, transport aircraft, helicopters, and ground forces on the move, and far too many were Chinese red instead of Indian blue.

"Holy shit," murmured Child. "It's actually happening."

Morrison headed for the door. "Keep me posted on Jack and the others. I need to talk to Washington to see what our response will be."

Leroux pointed at the tactical display, the lower-left including the Arabian Sea. "I think your answer is right there, sir."

Morrison stopped and cursed at the sight of dozens of green targets leaving Carrier Strike Group 5.

Child slumped in his chair. "Does this mean we're at war with China?" he asked, his voice tinged with fear.

Morrison regarded him for a moment. "I don't know, son, but I'm going to find out."

Indian Airspace

Dawson slowly shook his head as he read the update on the tactical situation, reading off the highlights to his team. It was depressing. Yet another war over nothing.

Niner tossed his head back. "You know, I'm not surprised that the Chinese invaded, yet I still am surprised. What the hell is up with these people? Why are we still fighting wars? What could China possibly hope to gain by doing this?"

Atlas shrugged. "Some people are still stuck in the past and think territory is everything. Look at Russia with Crimea, and now Ukraine. Or China with Taiwan or the South China Sea. We used to be the same way."

Spock cocked an eyebrow. "Maybe a century or two ago."

"Exactly. The United States was a rare democracy back then, competing with many countries that weren't. But now we've proven that democracy works despite its imperfections. Yet China and Russia are still stuck in the past, refusing to embrace a new way of coexisting. They still think they'll get more than they deserve through threats and intimidation, and sometimes outright war."

Dawson agreed, but there was no time for a philosophical debate. "We'll discuss that in the aftermath, but for now, what needs to be discussed is that our orders have changed. Senator Simmons is dead, as is his entire entourage." He quickly held up a hand, calming the shocked faces. "No, that entourage did *not* include our friends. Jack managed to get them out and they're in a vehicle headed west." Relieved sighs surrounded him, and he shared their relief. "Our orders now are to secure them and extract them, but only if necessary. If Jack can get them far enough away from the front lines, we might not be needed."

"And what are the chances of that?" asked Niner.

Dawson wagged the tablet with the tactical update. "If this is any indication, slim to none. The Chinese are pouring over that border and paratroopers are dropping all over the area. It's all going to depend on how deep into Indian territory they want to penetrate. For all we know, they could have already set up a blockade ahead of Jack's position. If they're captured, the question is, what are their orders, especially when they find a car full of Americans and Brits."

Jagger pursed his lips. "Something tells me that decision will be made by how our government reacts."

Spock gestured toward the windows. "Our escort is leaving us."

Dawson twisted in his seat to see the Indian fighter jets peeling off. The voice of their pilot, Captain Estevez, crackled overhead.

"I've just been informed that our escort is needed elsewhere. If you look out the port side, however, you'll see something that'll either make you smile or cry. I haven't decided which one yet."

Everyone headed for the left side of the aircraft and stared out the windows at the sight in the distance, and Dawson felt as Estevez did, uncertain as to how the prospect of dozens of American aircraft heading into a war zone should make him feel—pride in the bravery on display by the men and women racing into battle, or sorrow, knowing that many of his nation's finest might not be coming home.

Northwest of the Indian Army Northern Command Communications Center
Uttarakhand, India

Captain Kumar jerked back to consciousness with a huge gasp. His entire body ached, and he lay still for a moment as he assessed the damage. He could take full breaths, which was critical, suggesting his ribs were all right. He opened his eyes and was greeted with a close-up view of the rock-strewn landscape upon which he was lying face down. He could breathe, he could see, and he could hear the loose rock under him shifting as he moved. He wiggled his fingers and toes then pushed up onto his knees, relieved to find that nothing was broken, though he was badly bruised. When the Chinese missile had taken out the SAM, he had managed to dive behind a large rock, but the concussive force of the explosion had lifted the ground, tossing him in the air then slamming him back down, knocking him unconscious.

But he was alive.

He rose to his feet and shook his head at the sight of the SAM installation, completely destroyed, the wreckage still in flames. He activated his comms. "This is Zero-One. Everyone report your status, over."

He was greeted with silence then a groan to his right. He rushed over to find Raj lying on his side, a large shard of rock protruding from his back. Kumar dropped to his knees beside his comrade. "Just stay still. Let me take a look at you."

"Staying still is about all I can do," gasped Raj.

Kumar examined him for other wounds, but found none beyond the shard. Jet engines screamed overhead and they both stared up to see the Chinese crossing their skies unchallenged, at least in this location. With the SAM site taken out, there was no reason to target this location again, so they should be safe for the moment, though he couldn't be certain how long that would last.

"Please tell me that's not what I think it is."

Kumar peered back up at the sky and cursed as dozens of parachutes opened overhead. Footfalls behind him had him spinning and raising his weapon.

"Friendlies on your six!"

Kumar breathed a sigh of relief as Team Two appeared unscathed. He rose and pointed at one of his men, Muthu, an experienced medic. "Tend to Raj. We have to move." He pointed up at the paratroopers. "We're going to have company any minute now. Check the SAM, see if there are any survivors. Team Three was there helping them prep. I want to be out of here in five minutes."

Muthu looked up at him from Raj's side. "He can't be moved with this in him. It could act like a serrated blade inside his body with every step."

Kumar took a knee and examined the now exposed shard, Muthu having cut away the clothing surrounding it. "How deep does it go?"

"There's no way to know."

"It doesn't look like it goes very deep." He pointed at the entry point. "It's tapering fairly steadily in the exposed area."

"Again, no way to know. Just because it's tapering above the skin doesn't mean that what's under it continues to."

Raj cursed. "Just pull the damn thing out. Deal with the consequences later. If you leave it in, you can't move me, which means I'm going to die when the Chinese get here. If you leave it in and you do move me, you're saying I could die because it could slice me open inside. So just yank the damn thing out and see what happens."

"But it could kill you."

"I'm dead either way."

Muthu turned to Kumar. "What do you think?"

"I think he's got a point."

Raj growled. "Enough debate." He reached down and grabbed the shard, yanking it free. Blood gushed and Muthu cursed as he leaped forward and applied pressure. Raj held up the stone dagger, revealing the bloody tip, barely any of it having been below the surface. Raj shook it in front of Muthu's face. "Well, is that deep enough to cause problems?"

Muthu fell back on his haunches as he took the shard and examined it. "No, it shouldn't, not where it was."

"Good. Then let's get the hell out of here." Raj moved to get up when Muthu shoved him back onto the ground.

"Let me bandage you up first, you fool, then we'll go."

Kumar rose as Team Two returned, their somber expressions confirming what he already knew. Team Three was dead, as was the SAM crew. He snapped his fingers at Muthu. "Sixty seconds."

"I'm working as fast as I can."

Kumar stared up at the sky, praying for the wrath of the gods to vanquish their enemies, then dismissed his silent prayer as useless. Gods were not at play today. Only politicians. "Better make it thirty seconds."

Director Morrison's Office, CIA Headquarters

Langley, Virginia

Morrison sat in front of his laptop, the hastily-convened meeting almost exclusively attended by video call, happening less than ten minutes after the attack on the communications facility.

"Run it down for us, Leif. I understand you have information that the rest of us don't."

"Yes, Mr. President. The ceremony at the facility started forty-five minutes early. Within minutes of the new start time, the senator's chopper departed the facility and exploded several minutes later. Until a few minutes ago, we didn't know why. Our asset on the ground has informed us that the Indians arrested an impostor on the helipad about ten minutes before the chopper departed. It's our belief that the infiltrator planted a bomb or sabotaged the chopper somehow. We believe a decision was made to abort the proceedings, and the senator was evacuated on his chopper as per preestablished protocol."

Secretary of State Hanks interrupted. "Wait a minute. He got on a chopper that they thought might have been sabotaged?"

"We're assuming they didn't know, that there was some sort of communications breakdown. All we can say for sure is that the senator did board that chopper with his team, and it blew up several minutes later. As soon as that chopper blew up, the Chinese launched over forty cruise missiles across the border within less than three minutes. Several minutes later, six missiles destroyed the compound, presumably killing everyone who hadn't managed to escape, including, unfortunately, the infiltrator, who may have been able to answer some questions."

"So, we're assuming this infiltrator was Chinese or at least working for them?" asked the president.

"I don't see who else it could be," said Hanks.

Morrison replied. "We're assuming so, however, we don't know yet for certain. We're trying to reach our Indian counterparts to see if they have an identity for him, though we don't know if they're even aware of the arrest. Once we have that information, that should help us confirm that the Chinese sabotaged the senator's helicopter."

The president sighed. "That's a critical question that we need answered here. Until this moment, I wasn't aware of the infiltrator, so I ordered our air assets into the area to engage any Chinese air forces that might cross the border with the understanding that the Chinese had just shot down Senator Simmons' helicopter, a brazenly hostile act. Now you're telling me somebody on the ground might have done it, and there's a possibility, however remote, that the Chinese didn't."

Hanks threw up his hands. "And again, I ask, 'Who else?'"

Morrison chewed his cheek for a moment, having had little time to think about recent events. There was a disconnect here. Why would the Chinese intentionally kill the senator? And why would they use a bomb to do it when they could have blown the helicopter out of the air in half a dozen other ways that didn't rely upon Indian security failing? But an even more critical question was, why kill the senator at all? All that would do is antagonize America and possibly get them involved in the conflict. And there was no way China could want that.

He cleared his throat. "Mr. President, I think we do need to entertain the idea that someone else might be behind this."

Hanks leaned into the camera. "And again, I ask, for the love of God, who? Who could possibly want to get involved in this?"

"I'm not sure, Mr. Secretary, however, ask yourself this, why would the Chinese rely on an infiltrator to place a bomb on board the senator's chopper, when if they had every intention of killing him, they could have simply launched an air-to-air missile or taken him out from the ground using one of the teams they've already inserted. If they intended to kill him, the operation could have failed if their infiltrator was captured before he had time to plant the bomb. It makes no sense."

"Unless they wanted to sow confusion, like they apparently have succeeded in doing," replied Hanks. "Right now, they have us second-guessing whether they were even involved. For all we know, they did have a team in place, ready to take him down if their decoy infiltrator failed."

"Yes, Mr. Secretary, that's absolutely a possibility. And if we assume you're correct, the question that still begs an answer is why? Killing the senator doesn't benefit them in any way. At best, it pisses us off. At worst, we commit our forces, which we've already done."

"Perhaps I should have our forces stand down," said the president. "At least until we have this sorted out."

"Absolutely not, Mr. President!" protested Hanks. "We had already committed to sending our forces into the area the moment the Chinese crossed the border. This doesn't change anything. The Chinese have crossed the border, our allies require our assistance, and we need to send a message to the Chinese that this nonsense won't be tolerated."

"And what if they didn't kill the senator?"

Hanks sighed heavily. "With all due respect to Leif, have we considered the fact that maybe the Chinese were sending a message to us that they're not afraid to kill our government officials?"

Morrison leaned back in his chair. It was a possibility he hadn't considered, and Hanks was right. It was something he could see the Chinese doing. He leaned closer to the camera. "Mr. President, we'll continue to look into the situation, and the moment we have anything further, I'll let you know."

"Thank you, Leif. All things considered, whether it was the Chinese or someone else who killed Senator Simmons, they have crossed the border, and that was our trigger for sending in our air power. We'll continue with what we've committed to, and God help us all if the Chinese don't back down."

Indian Army Northern Command HQ

Udhampur, India

Colonel Mandal frowned as he listened to the latest reports read to him by the command center's coordinator. Senator Simmons was dead, and within minutes, the Chinese had sent missiles across the border, taking out the SAM installations, including some of those his Special Forces teams had attempted to secure. The Chinese teams had all been eliminated by his men, but the target coordinates were already in the hands of the Chinese, and there had been no time to move all the mobile installations.

All assessments had indicated the Chinese would cross the border unopposed in the air until the Air Force could respond, though his briefing suggested his country's air power would be quickly overwhelmed—it was essential the Americans be brought into the conflict, and with the death of the senator, that appeared to be happening. Their entry into the battle guaranteed victory in the end. Like his country's command, the Chinese undoubtedly believed the

183

Americans would stay out of it, letting China throw its weight around once again unopposed. Killing Simmons changed the equation, the brazenly brutal act something that couldn't go unanswered.

His phone vibrated in his pocket with a text message. He brought it up and tensed. The letters and numbers, which would appear to anyone else as a garbled message, were in fact a code that few knew, indicating something had gone wrong.

"I'll be back in a minute." He left the command center and swiftly strode to his office, resisting the urge to run. He closed the door, locking it behind him, then pulled his personal laptop from his briefcase, launching the secure messenger.

What is the problem?

The reply was instantaneous.

Asset on the ground was captured.

His tense muscles relaxed, for it didn't matter. The asset had completed his mission and planted the bomb on the senator's chopper, successfully taking him out and bringing the Americans into the conflict. He responded.

This is hardly news. His mission was accomplished. Don't contact me again unless there's a real emergency.

He was about to snap the laptop shut when it beeped with a reply.

This is an emergency. His picture and fingerprints were transmitted before the Chinese took out the installation.

He growled then typed.

We expected that, which was why we chose who we did.

Yes, but the Americans have requested everything that is known about him.

He slammed his fist against his desk, everything on it rattling in protest. How the hell had the Americans found out about the infiltrator? There had only been minutes between his arrest and the elimination of Simmons and his security team. And if they had known about the infiltrator, there's no way they would have boarded the chopper. So, who had told them? How had they found out?

He closed his eyes and inhaled, then sent his reply.

Burn it to the ground. I'll handle things on this end with the Americans.

Operations Center 2, CIA Headquarters

Langley, Virginia

Leroux watched the tactical display showing Chinese airpower flowing across the border unchallenged. The Pentagon was reporting paratroopers landing at critical points throughout the region, with the Indian Army unable to respond quickly enough as they couldn't use air assets to move their troops, and Chinese aircraft were strafing the roads.

In other words, things were going exactly as expected.

"Do we have an ETA on our aircraft arriving in the area?"

"The lead assets will be in position in twenty minutes," replied Tong. "The rest are doing a mid-air refuel in case they have to engage the Chinese for longer than expected."

"You're going to want to see this, Chris," called Therrien from the back of the room.

A live broadcast from the BBC snapped on the main displays, a shaky camera shot showing scores of Chinese tanks, armored personnel carriers, and transport vehicles rolling across the border. Dozens of dead

Indian soldiers were strewn about, their defensive positions now smoking ruins. A Chinese soldier rushed toward the camera and Leroux tensed for what was to come—the brutal treatment of yet another member of the press by the Chinese. But it wasn't to be. Instead, they were pushed to the edge of the road and allowed to continue reporting.

Child spun in his chair. "Well, I wasn't expecting that."

"Neither was I," agreed Tong.

Leroux dropped back into his seat, not realizing he had stood. "Their orders must be to leave the press alone. They must want positive coverage only."

Tong gestured at the screen. "I'm seeing an awful lot of dead Indians. I'm not sure how that's positive coverage."

"Dead Indians means victory, and to the Chinese, that's positive coverage. They just don't want any atrocities played out on the screen. They keep claiming the Indians are the aggressors here, and that any action they take is defensive only. Well, it's hard to defend that position if you're killing reporters and civilians."

Child stopped spinning in his chair. "Let's hope that extends to American and British citizens caught in the war zone."

Leroux was about to agree when his station beeped with an urgent message. He brought it up, finding a secure message from Morrison, the attached directory containing everything the Indians knew about the infiltrator. Leroux smiled. They were back in the game. He forwarded the message to everyone in the room then turned in his chair to face them. "Okay, people, I just sent you everything the Indians have on our infiltrator. I want every database checked. We need to know who this

187

guy is. I want to know who his family is, who his friends are, everything we can find out about him. In the meantime, I want his face mapped and run through every camera archive we have access to in the region. Scotty didn't beam him in there. He had to drive in or fly in. Let's start running him and do what we do best. I want to know why someone felt it was necessary to kill Senator Simmons and drag us into this war."

West of Indian Army Northern Command Communications Center

Uttarakhand, India

Laura drove, her skills behind the wheel never in doubt as Jack rifled through a suitcase in the back of the SUV. Acton occupied the passenger seat, leaning forward and peering up at the sky, already having lost count of how many airplanes had ripped past them. In the past fifteen minutes, they had already spotted several groups of paratroopers, so far all to the north and south, none ahead of them, though with the mountains towering all around them, there was no way to be certain.

"Okay, pull over," said Jack, finally done with whatever he was doing.

Laura glanced in the rearview mirror and yelped as she flinched, a hand darting to her chest before she laughed. "My God, Jack, if you're going to do something like that, at least warn us."

Acton turned around to see a middle-aged Chinese man in the rear row, wearing Jack's clothes, and his heart skipped a beat as well. "Holy shit! Definitely warn us next time."

189

Jack gave them both a look. "What? You thought some Chinese guy managed to get in the back seat at the speed we're going?"

Laura gently pulled them off to the side of the road then switched positions with Jack, Acton joining her in the rear row.

"I'll take the passenger seat," said Reading but Jack waved him off.

"No, I'm now your chauffeur." He hammered on the gas, sending them hurtling down the road once again before explaining. "If we encounter a Chinese roadblock, I might be able to bluff our way through if they think I'm one of them."

Acton eyed him. "You really think you're going to be able to bullshit your way through a roadblock in the middle of a war with a Halloween mask?"

"A state-of-the-art Halloween mask. And I've done it before. I'm very good at my job."

"And if someone decides to pull that mask off?"

Jack stared in the rearview mirror at him. "Professor, when's the last time you spontaneously thought to try ripping someone's face off?"

Tommy chuckled. "I think he's got you there, Doc."

Acton wasn't convinced, though he was certain of one thing—if the Chinese stopped a vehicle full of American and Brits, it likely wouldn't end well. If Jack could talk their way through a checkpoint, it just might save all their lives. "They'll kill you if they catch you."

Jack shrugged. "The moment you sign the contract to become an operations officer for the CIA, you've essentially signed your death warrant. Then you just hope you've made a liar out of yourself and survive to see retirement."

190

"I thought there was only a hundred-fifty-some-odd stars on the wall at CIA headquarters," said Tommy.

Jack glanced at him. "There are other ways to die, kid, where you can still have a pulse."

Tommy opened his mouth, his puzzled expression suggesting he was about to request an explanation when Mai squeezed his wrist and shook her head, silencing him. "I'll explain later," she whispered.

Laura took Acton's hand. They had so many friends now that did jobs like Jack's, including Acton's former student Dylan Kane, and the members of Bravo Team. If they survived long enough to retire, would they be dead inside, numb to the world because of all they had seen and done over their careers? Witnessing so much death, so much horror, had to have an effect. Acton could never count how many times he had prayed for the men and women serving his country, but the familiar refrain of peace on Earth, goodwill to all men, appeared fruitless. Here he was in a civilized country now at war with China, also a civilized country, the basic differences superficial in the grand scheme of things except for their types of government. One, the world's largest democracy, the other, the world's largest dictatorship.

Throughout modern history, no true democracy had ever attacked another, yet despite this, democracy was fundamentally flawed—it gave every idiot the right to vote. But as Winston Churchill had said, democracy was the worst form of government except for all those other forms that have been tried from time to time. Throughout history, all systems failed, not necessarily because the method of government couldn't work, but because someone else who didn't believe in what you

191

did came along that was stronger. Pax Romana lasted two hundred years, but the Roman empire eventually fell, leading to the Dark Ages where centuries of human potential were wasted.

Western democracies were slowly crumbling, political correctness gone mad combined with social media where anonymity reigned, had most people of good conscience and good character holding their tongue. The fact someone could have their life destroyed today because of a joke they told when they were twenty years old was ridiculous, for it assumed that people were incapable of change. Society evolved because the individuals of that society evolved, and eventually enough of them became a voice so loud that those stuck in the past were eventually dragged forward until that minority became a majority. There would always be some who could never move forward, who would cling to their bigotries, and those people perhaps deserved to be canceled.

But today, the ignorant of the woke culture somehow believed that everyone's past should be blemish-free, and he wondered how they would react someday when that photo of them enjoying a hamburger with their friends was used to cancel them in twenty years when everyone ate lab-grown meat because society had decided raising animals for slaughter was immoral. Too many of the woke crowd forgot that the societal norms of today were not the societal norms of fifty years ago, or even ten. That wasn't to say they were correct in the past, however entire generations can't be condemned for believing what the vast majority of those around them believed. If that were the yardstick now used to measure a person's worth, the next generation would surely condemn this new woke one for things it perceived were atrocities.

It was a vicious cycle that had to be broken, otherwise, the collapse of Western civilization would only be accelerated. He feared for the generation he taught, yet that was the very generation contributing toward the destruction of his way of life. They in no way had a monopoly on lunacy. His generation, and those of his parents, were gripped in a death struggle to show that only their beliefs were right, and anyone who disagreed was an evil moronic liar.

The binary society.

He sighed as he leaned his head against the window, more planes crossing overhead signaling the continued insanity gripping the planet, nearly three billion people now at war over an inconsequential piece of territory with nothing of value beyond bragging rights.

"Are you all right?" asked Laura quietly.

"Just thinking about how messed up this world is we live in."

"It is pretty messed up, isn't it?"

Jack pressed a finger against his ear then cursed. "Well, folks, it's about to get a little more messed up."

Operations Center 2, CIA Headquarters

Langley, Virginia

Child threw a hand in the air as he did a victory spin. "I found him."

Leroux turned. "Where?"

"On the footage the Indians just provided us from the communications facility."

"That's not very helpful," said Tong. "We already know he was there."

"Ah, but now we know how he got there."

Footage appeared on the screen, showing their target climbing out of a troop transport. Leroux rose from his chair. "When is this?"

"Four hours before the detonation. It was the shift change."

Leroux stared at the footage playing on a loop. "Okay, follow him, see if he interacts with anyone. I want to know if he had any friends inside. Find out from the Indians where those troops came from and see if we can get any footage. Sonya, do we have anything on this guy yet besides his name?"

She shook her head. "I've run his name through every database we have. He appears nowhere. As far as I can tell, this guy has never left India, which isn't necessarily out of the ordinary, but it doesn't help us much."

"And what have we got from the Indians? Do we have anything? Birth certificate, driver's license, whatever the hell they have over there that involves a government database?"

She shook her head. "The last update I have is they've come up empty. He's not in any of their databases."

Leroux's eyes narrowed. "That just doesn't make sense. They have to have at least something on this guy." He stared at the screen, searching for anything that might give them a clue. And he found it. "Watch how they jump out of the back of that truck."

Tong stared. "What am I looking for?"

"Anything out of the ordinary?"

The loop played repeatedly and Tong finally shrugged. "I don't see anything."

Leroux turned to the room. "Does anybody see anything out of the ordinary?"

Head shakes all around.

He stabbed a finger toward the screen. "Exactly. How many of you would jump out of the back of the truck without hesitation in exactly the same manner as every other soldier with you did? I know I'd be hesitating. Hell, I might even drop down on my bum and climb down.

J. ROBERT KENNEDY

But this guy walked right up, and when it was his turn, he jumped exactly like the rest."

Tong's jaw dropped. "He's a soldier!"

"Exactly. He's a soldier, and there's no way in hell if he's a soldier that he's not in their database. They've got his face, they've got his fingerprints, they've got his name. We can dismiss the name, but not the rest."

"Could they just not have found him yet? Maybe they're not as computerized as us," suggested Child.

Leroux shook his head. "You're forgetting one thing. What was the report from the Indians?"

Tong stared at him. "I must not be on my game today. What am I missing?"

"The Indians reported that they didn't find him in any of their databases. They didn't report that they hadn't found him *yet*. They reported he was not in their databases, so unless we're dealing with incredible incompetence—"

Child stopped spinning in his chair. "Holy shit! Someone's lying to us!"

Leroux snapped his fingers. "Exactly. Now we need to figure out who."

Therrien interrupted the revelation. "They're about to reach that roadblock."

All focus switched to the satellite shot showing the black SUV containing Jack and the others rolling up to a roadblock manned by a dozen Chinese paratroopers discovered only minutes ago. With a

196

Chinese convoy behind them, there had been no opportunity to avoid it and the decision had been made to let Jack attempt to bluff his way through.

Leroux said a silent prayer for them, though had a feeling that today, no one was listening.

West of Indian Army Northern Command Communications Center

Uttarakhand, India

Acton frowned as they drove past the smoldering wreck of a notorious British automobile. He peered through the smoke and it thankfully appeared empty. Whoever had once occupied it had escaped hopefully unscathed, but, unfortunately, it suggested the Chinese weren't to be trifled with.

"Why do you think they shot it up?" asked Tommy as Jack continued to approach the Chinese checkpoint, his speed barely a crawl.

Reading grunted. "Don't read too much into that, lad. That thing could have just decided to blow up on its own."

Acton chuckled and Jack snapped, "No joking. Everybody get your passports out and hold them up over your heads."

Mai gasped. "We don't have ours!"

"What?" cried Laura. "Why don't you have your passports?"

"I wasn't thinking. We left them in our bag. I just assumed we'd be leaving with the senator and we'd have time to collect them, and if there were an emergency, it wouldn't matter." She burst into tears. "I'm sorry. I'm not used to passports."

Tommy wrapped an arm over her shoulders. "It never occurred to me either. Don't blame yourself."

Jack glanced in the rearview mirror. "Okay, what's done is done. It doesn't matter now. If they ask, you tell them that exact story, that you're an American, born and bred. If we get into trying to explain your true history, it's just going to cause problems."

"But what about her accent?" asked Laura.

"She grew up in Little Vietnam and didn't get out much. Now, everybody pull yourself together. Keep your hands up, keep your mouth shut unless they ask you a question, then all you do is tell them the truth we discussed. You were supposed to leave with the senator but were left behind, and I offered you a ride. Don't try to get fancy with anything. It's okay to look scared. You should be scared. We're in the middle of a war zone and we have no idea if these guys are about to kill us. If you try to act brave or nonchalant, they'll pick up on that." He glanced in the rearview mirror as he came to a halt. "Hugh, you don't look scared enough."

Reading shrugged. "Because I'm not scared. If I die, I die. I've led a good life. Don't worry about me. Just do your job and we'll be all right."

"That's the spirit." Jack rolled down his window as they were surrounded, weapons aimed in every window. Acton applauded himself for having the foresight to go to the bathroom before all hell broke loose, otherwise, he might have pissed his pants. Someone in charge said something in Chinese and Jack responded in flawless Mandarin, handing over identification no doubt skillfully crafted by personnel safely ensconced in Langley. The ID was examined and more questions were asked, several finger jabs at the passengers causing them all to flinch with each one.

Particular interest was paid to Mai who, other than the disguised Jack, was the only non-Caucasian in the vehicle. Acton, sitting behind her, leaned forward slightly, his head directly behind hers so their interrogator couldn't see his mouth. He whispered, limiting his lip movement as much as possible. "Just remember, speak only English and don't worry about your accent. It's barely there anymore, and I doubt they'll notice."

She gave a single nod and he slowly leaned back. The guard shouted something and Jack held up his hands. "Okay, everybody. The captain wants us out. Just do what he says. Just stay calm and don't panic. They just want to search us and the vehicle."

The soldiers stepped back, their weapons still aimed at them. Doors opened on both sides and everyone stepped out. Reading was on the driver's side with Jack, the rest on the passenger side. Acton positioned himself between Laura and the soldiers, and when Tommy noticed, he did the same for Mai, who stood with her arms high in the air, her entire body trembling as she struggled to control the tears.

Gestures were made and Jack translated. "They want your passports."

Acton, Laura, and Reading handed them over, then one of the guards screamed at Tommy, no doubt demanding his identification. Tommy shook his head, his eyes bulging, his voice trembling. "I don't have my passport. I'm sorry. I forgot it."

A thought occurred to Acton. "Do you have your wallet?"

He nodded. "Y-yes, I do."

"Hand it over to them."

Tommy's hand darted to his rear pocket when the soldier stepped forward, raising his weapon, aiming it directly at Tommy's head.

"Slowly," said Acton. "He thinks you could be reaching for a gun. Turn so he can see your butt cheek."

Tommy slowly turned and leaned over slightly, exposing his back pocket. He reached in with two fingers and pulled out his wallet then handed it over to the impatient soldier.

"Mai, do you have your wallet?" asked Laura, her voice barely a whisper.

"Yes. It's in my clutch."

"Where's your clutch?"

"In the back seat."

Laura turned her head to see Jack. "Excuse me, sir, but my friend needs to get her purse from the back seat. It has her ID."

Jack translated for the soldier and he gave a quick nod.

"Go ahead. Slowly," repeated Acton as Mai turned a little too quickly. She inched into the cabin and emerged a moment later with her clutch held high. She opened it and handed over her own wallet. One of the soldiers collected all the identification and stepped away, pulling out a radio, reading off the particulars to whoever was at the other end, leaving Acton to wonder how good the communist state's intel was. If they had someone on the inside, did that someone have access to the guest list? Were they checking their names against it? And if they were, what would they do when they found Jack's alter ego wasn't on it?

And it was perhaps the revelation that he wasn't on the guestlist that had the man on the radio shouting something excitedly. The soldiers took several steps back, aiming their weapons directly at their prisoners.

"Well, I think this just backfired," muttered Acton.

Mai whimpered and Tommy paled.

"Everybody remain calm," said Laura in her soothing voice. "I think it's time we throw Jack under the bus."

Acton agreed. "Everybody sticks to the story. We don't know who the hell he is. He just offered us a ride and we took it in the panic. No matter what, we don't know him."

"Even if—" asked Tommy through clenched teeth.

Acton cut him off, knowing he was asking about the disguise. "Even if. Everybody will be just as shocked as these soldiers."

West of the Indian Army Northern Command Communications Center
Uttarakhand, India

Kumar led the way as the six remaining members of his team slowly headed to the busiest road in the area, all the while keeping a wary eye on the skies above and the rock-strewn landscape ahead. They had spotted parachutes and knew without a doubt that at least a platoon was in their former location and could be in pursuit. He held up a hand, bringing them to a stop by a brook trickling down from the mountain. "Everybody refill your canteens. Do whatever business you need to take care of. Downstream, please. And drink as much water as you can. We're taking five minutes. Five only."

His men alternated tasks with two always on guard as Kumar kneeled beside the makeshift stretcher holding Raj. He checked the blood-soaked bandage. "How are you feeling?"

"Like a true maharaja carried by his servants back to his palace after surveying his lands."

Kumar chuckled. "Well, I can see being wounded in battle hasn't improved your sense of humor."

Raj shrugged. "I've always found myself to be quite funny. Maybe it's your sense of humor that needs work."

Kumar patted his friend on the shoulder. "Any business to take care of?"

"None I'd care for you to see."

Kumar gave him a look and Raj sighed.

"Fine." Raj grinned. "The bladder's feeling a little full."

Kumar frowned then Muthu thankfully returned. "He says he has to pee."

"I'll take care of it, sir."

Kumar headed for the brook, but not before overhearing Raj apologize to Muthu. "I'm going to need you to get him out for me. But don't be scared. It's not a coiled cobra as you might think. It's just me."

"We shower together, asshole."

"So, you've been looking."

"Would you shut up? I'm working."

"Well, you're taking your sweet time about it."

"Because I'm trying to get out your little cobra, but I can't find him."

There was a thud and Kumar spun to see Muthu lying on his back and Raj's fist still clenched, and for the first time since the attack, everyone was laughing, including Muthu, who jabbed a finger at Raj.

"If you can lay me out like that, you can pull your own cobra out of your pants."

Raj laughed. "Of course I can. I just wanted to see if you would actually touch it."

Kumar laughed then paused. "Wait a minute. You asked me first."

"Well, it would have been a better story if I was able to say my commanding officer pulled out the little guy for me, but I'll settle for a medic."

Gunfire erupted, erasing the frivolity of the past few minutes. Kumar dropped to a knee, quickly surveying the area. They were at the end of the valley, but the mountains surrounding them had caused the gunfire to echo. "Where did that come from?" he asked the team. Everyone agreed it had come from the direction they were heading in, confirming his own suspicions. He pointed at two of his men. "Go check it out."

They both nodded then scurried toward the danger.

Kumar turned to Muthu. "How's his wound?"

"It's fine. The bleeding's stopped. When we get back to base, it'll just need to be examined to make sure nothing was left behind, then cleaned and packed. He'll make a full recovery. Probably take a few weeks though."

"So, if we leave him here, he won't die?"

Raj stared up at him from the ground. "Leave me here? What the hell are you talking about?"

"If we have to engage the Chinese over that ridge, I can't have two men carrying you."

Raj held up both arms. "Get me up."

Muthu batted them away. "Don't be a moron."

Kumar's lieutenant handed him a pair of binoculars. He pointed at the far end of the canyon where they had come from. "We've got movement."

Kumar peered through the glasses and cursed. The Chinese paratroopers that had dropped on the SAM site after it had been taken out were indeed pursuing them. He handed the binoculars back. "All right, that settles it. As good as Raj thinks he is, there's no way he's taking on a dozen paratroopers on his own."

"Agreed," said Raj. "But if I didn't have this wound, you could have counted on me, Captain."

Kumar rolled his eyes. "Get him up. Everybody stay low. They might not have spotted us yet. If we can get around that ridge, we might be able to keep it that way."

Raj was lifted and everyone quickly headed after the scouts sent out ahead. Kumar once again attempted to radio in for an update on their evac chopper, though as more planes raced by overhead, he already knew what the answer would be.

Things obviously weren't going well for his country, and they were on their own.

Chinese Roadblock

Uttarakhand, India

"You arrogant fool!" screamed the Chinese captain in charge as he gripped Jack's mask in his hand, the state-of-the-art creation coming loose after Jack took a series of blows to the face. "We are all Chinese Special Forces. We speak English just as well as you do. You weren't fooling anyone."

Jack wiped his lip, glancing at the blood on his hand, then shrugged. "It was worth a try."

The captain gripped the mask with a fist and shook it. "What are you? CIA?"

"Oh God, would I ever love to be CIA. Those guys are so cool and so good-looking. They can get any woman they want. Or man if that's your thing. And I bet if I were CIA, I wouldn't have been stupid enough to get caught."

The man smacked him with the mask. "Enough. You're CIA or you work for them. You're definitely not a civilian." He walked over to

Reading and stared up at the tall man, the seasoned law enforcement professional showing little emotion, none of it fear. "And you, what's your story?"

Reading indicated the man holding their identification. "Like it says on the passport, Hugh Reading. I'm an Interpol agent."

"Interpol? Why is Interpol here?"

"I could ask you the same."

The mask was slapped across Reading's cheek. "I'm asking the questions!"

Reading's chest expanded and his shoulders squared as he glared down at the man. "If you didn't have your gun and all your friends to back you up, this old man would be teaching you a lesson."

The captain smiled and began removing his equipment. "You think you're tough, old man?"

"Hugh, what are you doing?" cried Acton. "Just let it go!"

"Look to my left through those bushes," hissed Reading.

Acton turned and gasped. Half a dozen bodies riddled with bullets lay unnoticed, their attire suggesting they had been guests at the ceremony. Laura inhaled sharply, a hand darting to her mouth as she too spotted the victims that had likely been the occupants of the burnt-out car they had passed approaching the checkpoint.

The captain glanced over at the corpses as he placed his belt with his sidearm on top of the roof of the car. "If you win, I let your friends go. But if I win, you all join them."

As much as Acton loved his friend, there was no way he was winning. There was a 30-year age difference, and the soldier was a highly trained Chinese Special Forces officer. Reading didn't stand a chance.

"And what about your men?"

Something was snapped in Chinese to the others.

"What did he say?" asked Laura.

Jack translated. "He said, if the old man wins, let them go. Nobody interferes."

Reading slowly shook his head as he eyed the soldiers, their guns still aimed at everyone. "I might believe you if they all shouldered their weapons."

His opponent chuckled. "Very well, old man." Another order was barked and weapons were slung.

"Now, I hope you're all ready for this," said Reading, and Acton let go of Laura's hand as he noticed his friend had made eye contact with him while speaking the unusual words. Reading held up his fists. "Marquess of Queensberry rules?"

The captain's eyes narrowed. "What?"

Reading's right hand swept out, smacking the belt sitting on the rooftop, sending it sliding across toward Acton. Jack spun on his heel and headed directly for the closest soldier as Acton reached out and yanked the sidearm from its holster, flicking off the safety as he turned. Reading hauled off and decked his shocked opponent with a left that shattered his nose, leaving blood flowing down his face as he crumpled to his knees. Laura stretched out both arms and grabbed Tommy and Mai, dragging them behind the vehicle and onto the ground.

Acton found his first target and squeezed the trigger, quickly moving on to a second then third as the startled soldiers reacted. Reading continued to lay a beating on the captain as Jack reached his target and punched him in the throat then spun him around, using him as a human shield as gunfire erupted in his direction. He got a hand on the trigger of the slung Type 05 SMG and sprayed his opponents with lead as Acton continued to fire, counting his shots. He reached up and grabbed the belt from the roof, yanking it to the ground as he fired his last round. He ejected the mag and reloaded with one of the spares from the belt.

"James! Two o'clock!" warned Laura.

Acton caught the soldier in his peripheral vision and dove to his right, rolling on the hard pavement before firing three shots. Gunfire tore up the road in front of him and he ducked, covering his head uselessly, when two more guns suddenly opened up from a different direction. The Chinese gunfire abruptly redirected and Acton didn't bother checking why. He instead took the opportunity to scramble to his feet and get to the rear of their SUV with Laura and the others. He peered out from behind the bumper to see the half-dozen remaining Chinese splitting their attention between Jack and the two new guns that had entered the action. Reading's opponent cried out in terror, the outburst cut off before their friend joined them a moment later.

"What was that?" asked Laura.

"That was this old bastard's boot crushing someone's skull."

Mai's eyes bulged and she gasped. "You killed him?"

"He was going to kill all of us, but he got cocky."

Acton leaned out and fired at one of the remaining Chinese, taking him down, but unfortunately drawing return fire. He pointed in the direction of the bodies. "Get over there. You're too exposed here."

Laura didn't bother arguing, nor did Reading. Reading grabbed Tommy and Laura took Mai, and they rushed toward the shrubbery opposite the remaining Chinese position. Acton breathed easy as they disappeared from sight, then turned his attention to the gunfight, pleasantly surprised to see only two soldiers remained. He took advantage of the distraction and carefully aimed, firing two into the one closest to him. The soldier dropped, exposing his friend, who shook as repeated rounds slammed into his body from multiple positions.

And then there was silence.

Jack shouted. "Everybody hold your positions and keep your cover! We don't know who we're dealing with here!"

A voice shouted from the new position. "I'm Havildar Ansari, Indian Army! Identify yourself!"

"I'm Jack White, United States Senator Simmons' security detail. I have five civilians with me, Americans and British."

"Understood. Please lower your weapons and we'll approach."

"What do we do?" asked Acton.

Before Jack replied, something hit the ground that sounded nothing like a weapon. "We do what he says. Lower your weapon, but don't drop it."

Acton stayed behind the bumper and pointed his gun at the ground. Two soldiers appeared from behind some rocks about 100 yards away. As they approached, he breathed a little easier as these men were clearly not Chinese, and bore Indian insignia. They quickly checked the Chinese bodies before one of them approached Jack. "Mr. White, I'm Havildar Ansari. It appears we got here just in time."

Acton rose to see Jack talking to the man, a Chinese meat sack lying at his feet, untold rounds fired into him by his comrades in their desperate attempt to take out Jack.

Jack surveyed the carnage. "I think we had things under control, Havildar. A couple of more minutes and we would've won."

Ansari tossed his head back, roaring with laughter. "I have no doubt, sir, I have no doubt. And I apologize if we stole your glory."

Jack chuckled. "Apology accepted. I have four civilians hiding in the shrubs. Is it safe to bring them out?"

"Yes, of course."

Jack turned. "You guys can come out now."

Reading rose first, surveying the situation before beckoning to the others.

"What's your situation?" asked Ansari.

Jack indicated the SUV. "We used this vehicle to escape before the missiles took out the communications center."

Ansari's shoulders slumped. "So, they did take it out."

"Yes."

"Casualties?"

"Near-total, I'm afraid."

Ansari cursed and stared at the Chinese bodies surrounding them. "Hopefully, I'll get a chance to kill a lot more of these bastards before this is over."

"Perhaps. For now, my concern is getting these people to safety. What can you tell me about the situation in this area?"

Ansari frowned. "Not much, I'm afraid. We've had limited contact with Command. We don't want the Chinese tracing our signal. We have at least a platoon behind us."

"And to the west?"

"No idea, but I wouldn't be surprised if you're going to find more of this."

"What would you recommend?"

"I suggest you keep off the roads. If the Chinese don't already know about what just happened here, they're going to as soon as these guys miss a check-in."

"Staying off the roads means traveling by foot. We're not going to get anywhere if we're doing that."

"My unit commander will be joining us shortly. Perhaps he'll have an idea."

Acton stepped over to them. "What's your extraction plan?"

Jack extended a hand toward Acton. "Havildar Ansari, this is Professor James Acton. You have him to thank for at least half a dozen of these bodies."

The havildar gave him a curt nod. "Professor, we were supposed to be extracted by helicopter. However, as I'm sure you've already noticed, the Chinese have complete air superiority. Any chopper sent in would be taken down. Until our Air Force has a chance to respond, which I suspect will be any minute now, you're going to have to hole up somewhere and avoid any more encounters with the Chinese."

Acton scratched the back of his neck. "Some place to hole up? I may know the perfect place."

Indian Army Northern Command HQ

Udhampur, India

Dawson stepped out of the back of the Osprey, one of the cooler transport aircraft he had the privilege of flying in, its vertical takeoff and landing capabilities useful in situations like today, where they had just set down in a cleared parking lot at Indian Northern Command. If they had been in a Hercules, they would have been forced to land at the nearest airstrip before being transported here.

With the Chinese invading ahead of schedule, they hadn't had time to get into position to assist the professors. According to Clancy, American air assets were about to engage the Chinese, and until air superiority was reestablished, they didn't want a lumbering Osprey flying into the region. Instead, they had been redirected here. Their Clancy equivalent now walked toward them. Dawson and the others snapped to attention, delivering salutes.

The colonel returned the salute and extended a hand to Dawson. "I'm Colonel Mandal."

"Sergeant Major White, Colonel. It's a pleasure."

"Follow me inside. We'll get you situated and briefed on the current status of your people."

"Thank you, Colonel. It's appreciated."

They strode through the main doors of the complex ringed by sandbagged positions, gunners on high alert everywhere. It might be peaceful here, but the troops on the front line belonged to this command, and these soldiers knew it was merely the luck of the draw that they weren't on rotation at the front on this given day. Inside, they found what Dawson hoped was organized chaos, as opposed to plain old chaos. People were scurrying about in every direction, concern and determination mixed among the faces. They were at war, and he understood the emotion.

They were led into the bowels of the building and put into a large conference room. Food and water were brought in, and a few minutes later an officer entered and they all rose. He stood at the end of the table.

"At ease, gentlemen. I'm Captain Patel. I'm here to brief you on what little we know at this point. Several minutes ago, elements of one of our units sighted a group of civilians we believe are your people. When our men arrived on the scene, your friends were engaged in a firefight with a Chinese Special Forces unit, a fight they appeared to be winning, which makes me think your people aren't who you claim them to be."

Chuckles rounded the room and Dawson answered the captain's puzzled look. "Oh, they're exactly who they say they are, Captain. It's just that these are exceptional people. The two professors are SAS trained and have probably seen more action than most of the people under your command."

Patel stared at him. "SAS trained? How did they manage that?"

"Impossibly deep pockets," rumbled Atlas.

Another confused look.

"They're rich, Captain," explained Niner. "Filthy, stinking rich."

Dawson explained further. "The head of their private security is former SAS. He employs a lot of ex-Special Forces types, so he's been training them. Hand-to-hand combat, weapons, tactics. We've all fought beside the professors, and every one of us owes them our lives."

"I see. I look forward to meeting them."

"And speaking of that, do we have an exfil plan yet?"

"No, we lost contact with the unit as they were about to engage. In fact, we've lost all comms. We're trying to reestablish them now. Regardless, your air forces have just engaged alongside ours. Several of our SAM batteries managed to escape the initial attack, and we've kept them offline until now. The Chinese are about to receive one hell of a surprise in the next few minutes. It's our belief we'll reestablish air superiority within the next hour thanks to the help of your country. Once we have control again, we can send in a chopper." Patel's phone vibrated on his hip and he retrieved it then cursed. "I'm sorry, but I must see to something."

"Is there a problem?"

Patel hesitated before replying. "We now know why we've lost comms. The Chinese took out the two satellites that handle all communications for Northern Command."

217

Dawson's eyebrows shot up. "Are you kidding me?"

Patel wagged his phone. "I'm sorry, but I have to go. I'll have you updated as soon as I can, but something tells me your people will be getting better information than mine until we can switch everything over to our other satellites."

Patel left the room and Niner leaned forward, placing his elbows on the table. "I wouldn't want to be on the space station right about now."

"Me neither," agreed Atlas.

Niner gave him a look. "Dude, they don't make space suits that fit gorillas."

Atlas eyed him. "That's true, but they did put chimpanzees in orbit and I'm betting they still have those suits hanging around somewhere in case you wanted to go up."

Spock cocked an eyebrow. "Didn't we have some sort of seminar on this?"

Dawson sighed. "Yes, we did."

Jagger wagged a finger. "Yeah, but that doesn't apply here. This is a lover's quarrel, not a racism thing."

Niner and Atlas' heads both spun toward Jagger. "This is *not* a lover's quarrel," boomed Atlas.

Niner reached out and took the big man's hand. "It's true, we never quarrel. This is just a lover's spat."

Atlas jerked his hand away. "You do realize there's liable to be a camera in this room, and we're representatives of our country. We're supposed to be acting professionally."

"Fine." Niner leaned back in his chair, folding his arms in a mock huff. "Next time we're bivouacked together you're the inner spoon."

Atlas gave him the stink eye. "If that were the case it would literally feel like an actual spoon."

Spock tapped his chin then pointed at them. "So, when you two share a tent, you zip your sleeping bags together?"

They both stared at Spock, neither apparently certain as to what to say. Spock cocked an eyebrow. "Holy shit, you do!"

Dawson ended the exchange by holding up a hand and not giving his comrades a chance to dig themselves out, which he had no doubt would lead to more hilarity the next time sleeping arrangements were mentioned. "Focus, gentlemen. We have a bigger problem now."

Jagger nodded. "Yeah, I was thinking about that. If the Chinese have taken out the Indian communications satellites, then that could mean their Special Forces unit that's with the docs might not have comms anymore."

Dawson agreed. "Which means they won't have any support and will be looking for some place to hole up until they can get it. The question is, where?"

Approaching Skeleton Lake

Uttarakhand, India

Laura sat huddled with James and Mai on the passenger side of the middle row, the other side folded down to make room for the wounded Indian soldier she now knew was named Raj. Jack and Reading were up front and Tommy was squeezed in the rear row with the medic. The other four soldiers were on the running boards of their shot-up but still functional SUV. Her husband's idea was crazy, but she didn't see how they had any other choice. The Chinese dominated the area and they couldn't risk running into another checkpoint, as she had no doubt their identities had been radioed in as had a description of the vehicle they were in. The moment they were spotted, they would likely be shot.

"How much farther?" asked Jack.

James leaned forward. "It should only be a few more minutes then there'll be a turn on your right. It's not much of a road. It's not paved."

Captain Kumar knocked on the windshield in front of Reading. Reading leaned forward.

220

"What is it?" asked Laura.

"He wants us to look up."

James put down their window and they both leaned out. She gasped at the sight overhead. Contrails crisscrossed the sky and dark black smoke indicated several aircraft had been blown out of the air. There was no way to know whose, but this was a new development. She hoped it meant the Indians were finally mustering a stand.

"That's a good thing, isn't it?" asked Tommy. "I mean, they're fighting back."

Jack glanced at him in the rearview mirror. "Assuming those are Chinese that blew up, yes."

Laura faced the medic. "Is there some way you can find out?"

The medic regarded her for a moment. "Would it make a difference?"

"Of course it would make a difference. It would mean there's hope."

"There's always hope, ma'am. The last report I heard before our comms went dead was that our Air Force was being joined by the Americans and were about to engage."

Reading looked over his shoulder. "Any idea why your comms went down?"

"No idea. They're satellite-based so shouldn't have."

Tommy's eyes shot wide. "Maybe the Chinese shot your satellites down."

Raj pushed up on his elbows. "Can they do that?"

"Yeah, they did it a few years ago as a test. Blew up one of their own satellites, sent debris everywhere. It's still causing nightmares for satellites and the space station."

"Idiots," muttered James. "If they've done that again and taken out your satellites, it could cause chaos in orbit. That's what happens when there are no consequences for your actions."

Tommy grunted. "If I were Elon Musk, I'd take a few hundred of my Starlink satellites and use them to nudge every Chinese one into the atmosphere."

James chuckled. "Unfortunately for Elon, there would be consequences. You have to be a dictator with a nuclear arsenal to get away with shit like that."

"Hate to interrupt the Star Wars discussion," said Jack as he stared in his rearview mirror. "But we've got somebody coming up behind us fast." He punched the roof a couple of times and Kumar leaned forward. Jack jerked a thumb behind them. Everyone turned and Laura's heart leaped into her throat at the sight of a Mercedes sedan quickly closing the gap.

"Could they have come from the communications facility?" asked Tommy. "Maybe they're just trying to get away like we are."

"No, if they had come from the facility, they would have caught up with us at the checkpoint."

James disagreed. "Not if they went the other way then changed their mind."

"Either way, the Chinese could have intercepted them and commandeered the vehicle. Those paratroopers didn't drop in with a luxury car dealer's inventory."

"What are we going to do?" asked Mai, her voice quivering with fear.

Reading pointed ahead. "We're going to floor this thing and get to that turn. If they've got any sense, they'll keep going."

Jack gave Reading a look. "If you think this beast carrying twelve adults is going to outrun that Mercedes, I want some of what you're on."

James pointed ahead. "It doesn't matter. There's the turn."

Jack took his foot off the gas and gently applied the brakes, not wanting to throw off their hangers-on. He made the turn then quickly regained speed. Laura stared out the rear window, her heart hammering, waiting to see what the black sedan would do, then bit her finger as it made the turn to follow.

"Well, that answers that," muttered Jack.

And if anyone was wondering whether the Indian Special Forces team had any doubts, they were answered the moment gunfire rang out from the four men clinging to the sides of the vehicle. The Mercedes swerved but the driver maintained control.

Then James shouted, "Everyone down!"

Laura ducked, covering Mai as James threw his body over both of them, the weapons she had caught a glimpse of as they emerged from the windows of the Mercedes now firing.

"How much farther?" shouted Jack as he battled to control the vehicle on the winding dirt road.

"We should be entering the valley any moment now," replied James. "When you do, turn to the right. Along the side—" He stopped, his jaw dropping as he stared ahead. Laura turned and gasped at the sight of a missile streaking into the sky.

Then she remembered the mobile SAM site.

And her heart sank as she realized they were heading directly toward a primary target.

Operations Center 2, CIA Headquarters
Langley, Virginia

Leroux stared at the displays, too many of them blank. "Switch birds. There has to be something that still has an angle on that area."

Tong threw up her hands. "I'm trying, but it's a cluster—" She held her tongue. "It's a mess up there. I don't know what's been taken out or what's just repositioning, but those two satellites they blew up have disrupted the entire region."

Leroux growled in frustration. "This is why we can't have nice things. Okay, keep searching. We need to find out where the professors went. Start mapping out the possibilities. They're probably going to want to get off the main road. Where else could they go?"

Child spun in his chair. "There are not exactly a lot of roads in this area." He brought up a map, throwing it onto the main display. "It's all mountains, so all the roads are going through the valleys. There's not exactly a lot of places for them to go."

Leroux stared at the map. Child's assessment was correct. The road the professors were on continued winding west, with few others branching off from it that led to anywhere significant.

"We're back online," announced Tong as one of the dead screens sprang back to life.

"Show us their last known position."

Tong tapped at her keyboard and the image resolved to the Chinese roadblock. Bodies were strewn about and Leroux tensed.

"Are any of those our people?"

The computer isolated the bodies, showing zoomed-in images. "It looks like twelve Chinese and four or five people, likely Indian, off to the side of the road."

Leroux rose and stepped toward the screens, his hands on his hips as he pieced together what he was seeing. He pointed at the civilians. "Check the earlier footage. See if those bodies were there and we just missed them." He waved a hand at the dozen dead Chinese scattered about. "This doesn't make sense."

"What do you mean?" asked Child.

"It looks like they were ambushed. If they were, it had to be by Indian soldiers, and they would have cleared the road. Instead, we've got bodies all over the place. Whoever did this left in a hurry. And where's the SUV? It hasn't even been ten minutes."

Tong pulled up an image showing the bodies in the bushes. "They were there already."

"Looks like we just missed them. We were too focused on the professors."

"Then what happened?"

Leroux pointed at the still-smoldering wreck of a car. "My guess is that this belonged to those people. The Chinese killed them, put the bodies out of sight, then the professors came along. Then..." He paused, waving a hand again at the carnage. "And they did this?" He shook his head. "How the hell did they take out a dozen Chinese soldiers?"

"They *are* trained," said Tong. "It wouldn't be the first time they've done the unexpected. Plus, Jack's with them."

Leroux shook his head. "They don't have weapons. Jack might have a Glock or something, but even he's not that good."

Child laughed. "He'd probably disagree with you there."

"Something must have happened that allowed them to get weapons at some point."

"Could they have had help?" asked Tong.

Leroux peered at the location of the bodies with respect to where they had last seen the SUV. He spotted something. "Wait a minute. Upper right quadrant. Zoom in on those bodies there." Tong dragged her mouse and the image zoomed in. Leroux snapped his fingers, a smile spreading as he pointed at the screen. "They had help."

Tong leaned forward, squinting. "What makes you say that?"

"Look at the blood spatter on the pavement."

Tong continued to stare, as did everyone else in the room. Child was the first to get it. "Holy shit! The spatter goes toward where the SUV would be. That means the gunfire had to come from the other direction."

227

Leroux gave a thumbs-up. "Gold star for Mr. Child. Somebody helped them, and that had to be Indian soldiers. And the fact that nobody's there anymore suggests they all left together."

"So then, they're safe?"

Leroux shook his head. "They're still in the middle of a war zone." He pointed at the tactical display showing the combined Indian and American fighter jets along with surviving Indian anti-aircraft batteries decimating the Chinese air forces, a tally on the right showing estimated losses of airframes for all three combatants, the American and Indian numbers thankfully in single digits with the Chinese already over fifty. "By the looks of things, we'll have air superiority very shortly, which means we'll be able to get choppers in to extract our people."

"What the hell is that?" exclaimed Therrien, and Leroux's heart leaped into his throat as hundreds of targets appeared on the far right edge of the tactical display.

"Start projecting where those missiles are heading. It looks like the Chinese aren't going to give up without a fight."

Tong gasped and Leroux spun toward her. "What?"

Her mouth was agape. "I just got the file on our infiltrator, and I think I know who's been lying to us!"

Skeleton Lake

Uttarakhand, India

Jack cursed as the road made a sharp turn. He slammed on the brakes, cranking the wheel to the right, sending them into a skid and the two soldiers on the driver's side tumbling.

"There it is!" shouted Acton, pointing toward the taped-off entrance to the cave.

Jack steered them toward their destination. "Everybody get ready!"

Acton glanced over his shoulder to see the two soldiers that had fallen off, sprinting after them, and the black Mercedes spinning out on the turn, buying them some time.

"Here we go!" shouted Jack as he slammed on the brakes, bringing them to a halt directly in front of the entrance. Acton threw open the door and jumped out, then helped Laura, Tommy, and Mai down.

"Get in the cave now! Go as deep as you can!"

"But won't they just follow us?" asked Mai.

"Just go!"

Laura grabbed Mai and Tommy, hauling them through the entrance, and Acton spun as another surface-to-air missile streaked off the weapons platform positioned nearby. He spotted Major Singh and pointed at the Mercedes. "Major! Chinese!"

Singh spun, noticing them for the first time, and held a hand up to his ear. "What?"

Acton pointed again at the car. "Chinese!"

Singh's eyes bulged and he started barking orders as yet another missile launched, blasting out of the valley and up into the sky. Reading and the medic carried the injured Raj through the cave entrance as Kumar and Jack directed weapons fire toward the Chinese, providing cover for those who had fallen off the SUV.

Jack cursed. "That thing's up-armored."

Kumar agreed. "I noticed that. It must have belonged to a VIP guest."

Another missile streaked from the SAM site as several of Singh's troops joined the gun battle. Acton spotted something that had his stomach churning. "Is that guy on a radio?"

Everyone held their fire for a moment and peered toward the Chinese. Jack repositioned slightly, opening fire once again. "He is."

"How long do you think it would take for reinforcements to get here?" asked Acton.

Jack shook his head. "He's not calling for reinforcements."

Kumar glanced over at the mobile SAM site. "He's calling in an airstrike."

Acton's eyes bulged. "Oh shit! How long will that take?"

"If it's delivered by one of their planes overhead? Seconds."

The rest of Kumar's team finally reached them and Kumar glanced over his shoulder at Acton. "All right, Professor. We're here. Now what's your plan?"

A shiver washed over Acton, for this was his plan. He had brought them here. He had committed them to this course of action. But this wasn't his plan. The Chinese were never supposed to be here, were never supposed to have followed them. They were supposed to come here, hide in the cave that no one knew about, then when things calmed down, call for help. But now the Chinese knew precisely where they were, a missile was likely inbound, and more troops would soon arrive.

They were screwed.

His heart hammered as a thought occurred to him. "I've got an idea, but you're not going to like it."

Indian Army Northern Command HQ

Udhampur, India

An alarm sounded and Dawson shot to his feet, as did the others. Shouts erupted on the other side of the closed door, whatever the alarm represented triggering an increasing panic.

"That sounds rather ominous," said Niner.

Dawson pointed at the door. "Check what's going on."

Atlas stepped over to the door and hauled it open, poking his head outside. "It looks even more nuts than before." He reached out and grabbed somebody, dragging them into the room. The startled man's hands shot up at the sight of six Delta operators in full combat gear. Dawson held up a hand to calm the man, and Atlas let go of the shirt he was gripping.

"What does the alarm mean?"

The man gulped. "It means we're under attack. Missiles are inbound."

Dawson cursed. "ETA?"

"Less than five minutes."

Dawson pointed at the door. "Everyone, let's go." He activated his comms. "Osprey Two-Niner, this is Bravo Zero-One, do you read, over?"

Estevez replied immediately. "Affirmative, Zero-One. What's your status?"

"We're evacing now. Power up the bird. We're leaving the moment our boots are off the ground. Missiles are inbound. ETA, five minutes."

"Roger that, Zero-One. Powering up. Try to put a wiggle on, would you? This beast is going to use up some of those five minutes just to get off the ground."

"Copy that. Wiggling. Zero-One, out."

Captain Patel sprinted toward them and skidded to a halt, beckoning them to follow. "Let's go! Let's go! We have to get you out of here now."

They raced down the corridor and Dawson caught up to Patel. "Do you guys have a hardened shelter?"

"We do, but apparently the Chinese have sent dozens of missiles toward us, probably in retaliation for taking out so many of their aircraft in the past few minutes. If even a few of those are bunker busters, nobody's surviving this, so we're doing as rapid an evac as we can to save as many of our personnel as possible."

"What about the colonel?"

"I saw him by the entrance coordinating things."

Dawson's comms squawked in his ear. "Bravo Zero-One, Osprey Two-Niner. Command confirms ETA until first impact four minutes, I repeat, four minutes, over."

"Copy that. If we're not there in time, you leave without us."

"Nuts to that, Zero-One. Just get your asses in gear."

Dawson chuckled. "Careful, Osprey Two-Niner, you just might make this grunt like a Navy boy." Estevez laughed as Dawson came into the main lobby of the building with the others. "Osprey Two-Niner, we'll be there momentarily. Zero-One, out."

Patel pointed ahead. "There's the colonel!"

Dawson spotted the man leaving through the main entrance and his eyes narrowed at the action. Why would a senior officer abandon his post while scores of his people remained?

Apparently, Patel had the same thoughts. "Where's he going?"

Dawson shoved through the doors and sprinted toward the Osprey, its massive rotors powered up several hundred yards away. "ETA to first impact, two minutes," came the report over his earpiece.

"Two minutes, people!"

Everyone sprinted hard. Spock and Jagger reached the ramp first and disappeared inside. Dawson kept pace with Patel and stopped at the ramp, turning to see the swift Niner lagging back with the lumbering Atlas. He beckoned them. "Let's go! Let's go!"

Niner reached over and smacked Atlas' ass. "Come on, beefcake, get those sweet cheeks moving!"

"Touch my ass again, little man, and I'll snap you like a wishbone."

Niner surged ahead. "Only if you can catch me."

Atlas growled and poured on a little more speed then rushed up the ramp after his friend. Dawson spotted Colonel Mandal climbing into an SUV, the vehicle speeding away the moment the doors closed. Dawson couldn't imagine Clancy doing anything of the sort, but there was no time for judgment now. "Let's go!" he shouted as he stepped inside the aircraft, and moments later it lifted off, the roar of the engines thunderous as the massive rotors lifted the 33,000-pound airframe into the sky. The ramp slowly rose and sealed them inside as Estevez's voice came over the speakers.

"Grab onto something. This could get rough."

Everyone not already in a seat rushed toward one. Dawson sat and grabbed the straps to buckle in when a terrific explosion overwhelmed the pounding of the rotors. He twisted around to peer through one of the windows and a lump formed in his throat as a massive fireball erupted into the sky, scores of personnel still streaming from the entrance and racing away from the complex.

He caught a brief glimpse of the next missile before it too slammed into the building, followed by two more as the Osprey continued to gain altitude, buffeted by the blast waves. Everyone watched in silence as the rotors slowly tilted forward and they put some distance between them and the danger that lay behind, detonation after detonation rumbling in their wake, buffeting the aircraft.

Sealing the fate of so many stationed at Indian Northern Command.

Operations Center 2, CIA Headquarters

Langley, Virginia

Leroux reread the files that Tong had discovered. The photo on the personnel record matched that taken of the infiltrator—there was no doubt this was the same man. He had served under Colonel Mandal's command for over five years until he was dishonorably discharged three months ago when it was revealed he was a Kashmiri separatist sympathizer. But if that were the case, why had any of this been hidden? He had already confirmed that Mandal was coordinating the investigation into the infiltrator and that he had signed off on the report indicating they had found no records of the man.

It was a lie.

The question was why? Was it because Mandal was involved, or was it something more innocent, such as protecting the Indian Army from embarrassment?

"It can't be that they're trying to cover things up to protect themselves," said Child. "It doesn't make sense. They have to know we'd eventually find out."

Tong turned in her chair to face him. "You're saying 'they.' For all we know, it's only the colonel. His superiors probably don't know, and his underlings wouldn't know if he's filtering their findings."

"So, he's protecting himself from embarrassment?"

She shook her head. "That's not what I'm saying. We don't know what his motives are. I'm just saying he could be acting alone."

Leroux pursed his lips as he faced the conversation. "There's only one way to know for sure."

"What's that?" asked Child.

"We need to see if there's anything that connects those two after he was dishonorably discharged. The colonel's movements are a lot easier to track because of who he is. Sonya, how did you find the record?"

"The Indians granted us access to all their personnel files the moment we committed our armed forces."

"So, we have access to everything from a personnel perspective?"

"Yes, sir."

"Then let's start pulling files on all of the officers under his command. If there's a conspiracy here, then he would need help. Start running their faces through all our databases." He twigged on something. "Wait a minute." He spun back toward his station, quickly bringing up Mandal's file. He tapped the screen. "Phone numbers. Check the phone numbers. See if these are landlines or cellphones, and pull everything we can for the past forty-eight hours."

"Just give me a second." Tong's fingers flew over the keyboard. "There are three numbers listed for him here. One's a home phone landline, one's his office landline, and the other is a mobile, looks like government issue."

"See if you can get phone records for all those numbers." He turned in his chair to face Child. "Can you get me any text messages sent or received by that phone?"

Child shrugged. "Sure, but it's going to take time. If I had it in my hands, I could access it a lot easier."

Leroux regarded him for a moment. "What if I could get it into someone else's hands?"

"It depends on how secure his phone is. A few seconds, a few minutes. Something tells me, though, that he won't want to hand it over."

"Could you do it through a cellular connection?"

"Depends on how secure it is, but I should be able to. I can force a carrier tagged update—"

Leroux held up a hand. "I don't need the instruction manual. Just do it. We need to know if he's been texting anybody."

"Got it." Child went to work as the door to the operations center hissed open and Morrison entered, his head shaking the moment his eyes were drawn to the screen showing satellite footage of the leveled Indian Northern Command Headquarters.

"My God. That's definitely an escalation."

Leroux rose. "It is. It's rather disproportionate, and it's not just their headquarters. The Chinese leveled pretty much anything associated with the Indian military within Northern Command. The casualty count is going to be in the hundreds, if not thousands. I guess they were pissed to lose their air superiority so decided to show they didn't need it."

Morrison indicated the tactical display showing few red targets, most of them either on the Chinese side of the border or rapidly retreating toward it. "With air superiority, we should be able to get people in to retrieve the professors."

Leroux chewed his cheek for a moment. "That might be, however, we have no idea where they are right now."

Morrison's eyebrows shot up. "Excuse me?"

"When the Chinese took out the Indian satellites, they damaged a couple of ours. SATCOM immediately began repositioning anything in the area. We were down for almost ten minutes. By the time we got back online, they were no longer at the Chinese checkpoint. All we found were dead Chinese, and the SUV was gone. We think they received help, most likely from the Indian Army, but we didn't spot them either."

"Where would they go?"

"We're not sure yet, but we're trying to find them. There's something more critical, though."

"What?"

"We believe Colonel Mandal might be involved in this situation."

Morrison cocked an eyebrow and folded his arms. "Explain."

"We've discovered that the infiltrator was under his command for years until he was dishonorably discharged only a few months ago. We're trying to see if there's any connection between the colonel and the infiltrator since then, either directly or indirectly through associates."

"But I thought the Indians said he wasn't in their records."

"That's what they said, sir. But all that information was fed through the colonel. He would have had the opportunity to change any reports before it got to us."

Morrison's head bobbed slowly. "Agreed, however, it could have been changed before it reached him or after it left him. We have to be careful here before we accuse an Indian Special Forces colonel of being involved in killing a US senator."

"We're trying to confirm it now, sir. Sonya is pulling his phone records and Randy is attempting to access his cellphone."

"Good. Let me know what you find. But why would he be involved? Why would he want to kill Senator Simmons?"

Leroux indicated his workstation's screen where he had reviewed the personnel file of the infiltrator. "Our suspect was dishonorably discharged for being a Kashmiri separatist sympathizer. It could have something to do with that."

Morrison scratched his chin then shook his head. "Doesn't make sense. It's too coincidental."

"What do you mean?"

"I mean, the Kashmiris decide to kill the senator…" Morrison's voice drifted off and he wagged a finger as a new thought occurred to him. "Wait a minute, wait a minute. It does make sense. It's too coincidental unless it's all connected. How does a dishonorably discharged Kashmiri get the explosives necessary to blow up the helicopter?"

"From terrorists?"

"Yes, possibly, but how does he get on the facility?"

"We know he came in on a troop transport with other soldiers."

"Right, so how did he get on the base? Where did he get the fake ID that was sent to us initially?"

"Kashmiri sympathizers," suggested Child as he continued to work.

"Possibly. And if that were true, the Indians have a much larger problem that they're going to have to deal with after this is done. But think about it. He had to smuggle the bomb onto the base and keep it on his person in the transport, then into the facility, then up to the helipad."

Leroux's head slowly bobbed. "It's possible."

"Absolutely. Or is it more likely it was already in position? Either on the base or at the facility?"

Leroux pursed his lips as he thought. "It would definitely be less risky."

"I agree. However, it's still possible for him to have smuggled the bomb the entire way on his own."

"And the terrorist group, depending on their capabilities, could have faked his identification."

"Agreed."

Leroux shook his head. "I don't understand, sir. Where are you going with this?"

Morrison chuckled. "That famous gut of yours isn't giving you any clues?"

"I'm afraid not, sir. It seems you're suggesting that Kashmiri separatism is behind Senator Simmons' death, but what would be the motivation?"

Morrison smirked. "What happened within minutes of the senator dying?"

Leroux's jawed slowly dropped. "Ahh! The Chinese attacked."

"Exactly. If I'm the Chinese and I'm rattling my saber like crazy, I'd pre-position troops to take out SAM sites in case I decide to invade. But the entire time I'm waiting to see what the senator says or does, just in case I want to change my mind. Then he's suddenly blown out of the sky. What do I do?"

"You invade?" Leroux was doubtful. "But why?"

"You're going to be blamed regardless. Nobody is going to believe you weren't responsible for bringing down the chopper, so you initiate the plan."

"Okay, so the Chinese trigger their attack because they think they're going to be blamed. Or, they could've planned on attacking regardless. But what's the Kashmiri's motivation? Why kill an American senator?"

"It brings another chair to the table." Tong's fingers paused for a moment. "They want their independence. Now, the United States is sitting at the negotiation table with their representatives and India."

Morrison jabbed a figure at her. "Exactly! That's exactly what they want us to think."

Both Tong's and Leroux's eyebrows shot up. "Sir?" asked Leroux.

"Think about it. It's ridiculous. Killing a US senator doesn't gain you support from America for your independence. If America were to sit at that table and negotiate with a position suggesting we favored Kashmiri independence, it'd be open season on our diplomats. Every nutbar group out there who thinks they should have their own little corner of their

242

country would be killing our people." He held up a finger. "But, if I'm the Indian government, and a government representative of one of my strongest allies and most important economic partners just got blown out of the sky by Kashmiri separatists, what do you think my reaction would be?"

"I'd want to deal with the problem once and for all."

"Exactly."

Leroux leaned against the station. "So, if we assume the colonel is involved, this isn't about the Chinese at all, this is about Kashmiri independence. He's using this situation with China to force his government into acting once and for all to deal with the problem."

"I'm willing to bet you that there's something in his past that has him hating the Kashmiris for some reason. He takes one of his men who's loyal to the country, but happens to be from Kashmir, dishonorably discharges him, and now he has a pawn that he can use as needed. He's planning an attack on the communications facility, probably a bombing at the reception, but when it's announced that the senator will be there, he changes his plans. The bomb gets placed on the senator's chopper knowing that killing Simmons will demand a more vigorous response than just a bunch of locals would because of who he is. He has access to all the information, all the security details, everything to make the attack possible."

Leroux exhaled loudly, his lips vibrating. "It's thin, sir."

Morrison chuckled. "Razor thin. It's a theory with no proof to back it up."

"I might have something that proves your theory." Therrien pointed at the displays. "I've been running the colonel's face through our databases, and look what came up." An article from the Hindustan Times appeared, the headline emblazoned across the top of the page.

Funeral Held Today for Victims of Terrorist Bombing.

"Check this out." Therrien zoomed in on the featured photo of a funeral, then isolated one of the men standing with what appeared to be the family, his dress uniform indicating he was a lieutenant. "Anybody recognize this young man?"

Leroux's eyes widened. "Is that our colonel?"

"Yup. *Lieutenant* Mandal's family was killed in a bombing by Kashmiri separatists twenty years ago."

Child spun in his chair. "There's your motive. He wants his little war to be blamed on the same people that killed his parents so that his government has an excuse to go in once and for all and wipe them out."

Leroux bit his lip as he contemplated Child's theory. It was plausible, and if he wanted to, he could easily lose himself down the conspiracy hole too many people these days found themselves dwelling in by taking a single fact then attaching all sorts of conjecture to it to turn it into a theory that fit their narrative, no matter how ridiculous.

"What are you thinking?" asked Morrison.

"That we have to be careful." He glanced at Child. "Get me those text messages. Ignore our conversation." Child gave him two thumbs-up and a grin then set back to work as Tong returned to her keyboard to pull the phone records of the landlines. "We know the colonel's parents were killed by Kashmiri terrorists when he was younger, just starting out in the military. We know three months ago that someone under his command was dishonorably discharged for being a sympathizer. We know that this same man somehow infiltrated the facility with or without help, and planted a bomb on the senator's chopper. We also know that the initial information the Indians provided us was false. As far as I can tell, those are the only facts we have."

Child raised a hand as the other kept working his keyboard.

Morrison eyed him. "This isn't primary school. Say what you have to say."

"Well, while I'm attempting to get into this guy's phone, I also initiated a pull of all of his incoming and outgoing numbers." Child bent his wrist and pointed a finger at the displays. "The system is crosschecking everything now," he said as the screen filled with phone numbers. "But I think that top number should be of interest if we're trying to come up with theories as to what's going on."

Leroux squinted at the screen. "Wait a minute. Are you telling me that he received a text message that originated in China a few minutes ago?"

Child spun in his chair, his hands in the air in victory. "Yep, and look at that time code. It was sent two minutes before they launched that counterstrike."

Morrison whistled. "Are we suggesting that Colonel Mandal is not only trying to frame the Kashmiris for the murder of the senator, but is also in bed with the Chinese?"

Leroux clasped his hands behind his neck. "Something doesn't fit here. He frames the Kashmiris because he wants his government to go in and deal with them once and for all—that I can accept. But I read his file. Everything indicates he's loyal, but if he's working for the Chinese, helping them invade, it doesn't really fit. It weakens his country."

Morrison pinched his chin between his thumb and forefinger. "We've been trying to figure out why the Chinese are overreacting, why they're making such a big deal out of a communications facility of which they have three of their own on the opposite side of the border."

Tong turned in her chair. "I know I'm supposed to be working on the phone records, but what if he's feeding them false intel?"

Leroux and Morrison both faced her. "Explain," said Morrison.

"If he is loyal to his country, he has to think the Kashmiri threat is greater than the Chinese threat. He's been plotting his revenge probably for the past twenty years. Tensions are already high along the border. He knows that the communications facility, when it opens, will ramp it up even more, and his command is responsible for security, so he takes advantage of that. He and whoever else are involved choose a man they can trust, who's willing to sacrifice himself for his country. He's discharged as a sympathizer. They insert him into the facility, likely to bomb the reception that's been planned for months. But Kashmiris have committed terrorist attacks before and it's never resulted in the outcome he wants. He knows it has to be bigger, so he makes contact with the Chinese, starts feeding them false intel, perhaps about the facility, about India's plans in the region, that it's perhaps the first step toward an Indian incursion across the disputed border region. Anything to get the Chinese riled up enough to actually cross the border. Look at when the buildup began. It was only a couple of weeks after this guy was discharged."

An eyebrow shot up Leroux's forehead. "I hadn't thought of that, but you're right, that timing is pretty coincidental."

"So, he gets the Chinese riled up. They decide they have to send a message to India. He has his man kill the senator because he's a bigger target than the dignitaries, and when the dust all settles, I have no doubt he'll have planted information that makes it look like the sympathizer was the one coordinating with China. India will augment its capabilities at the border then they'll go into Kashmir and root out the separatist movement once and for all, and Colonel Mandal gets his revenge."

Morrison's head slowly bobbed. He turned to Leroux. "What do you think?"

"I think it's a perfectly sound theory all based on a single text message that we don't know the contents of, originating from China. For all we know it could've been a scammer telling him he just won a cruise and all he has to do is provide his credit card number."

Morrison sighed. "We have to get in that phone."

"We have to get in that phone."

Child waved a hand in the air. "I'm working on it, I'm working on it. But he's got some serious security on this thing, and half the cellphone towers in the area went dead with the attack."

Morrison cursed. "We need to know. People are dying out there, including our own men and women, in a war that quite possibly shouldn't be happening."

"Why don't we just grab it?" suggested Therrien.

Leroux glanced over his shoulder at the senior analyst. "What do you mean?"

"Find the colonel, aim some guns at his head, take the phone and see what's on it. We're at war. We could be looking at World War Three if things get out of hand." He pointed at the DEFCON indicator on the wall. "We're already at DEFCON Three, I'm seeing reports of the Chinese mobilizing forces across their entire territory, and naval assets deploying in the Pacific. And what are we doing? We're responding. This could quickly spiral out of control. I say hunt this mother down, get his damn phone, and see what it says. If it turns out he's innocent, we apologize and send him on his way."

"What if he's not?"

"Don't you think we should know that?"

Morrison thought for a moment. Leroux opened his mouth to offer his own thoughts but Morrison cut him off with a raised finger. The Chief continued to no doubt mull the consequences of what Leroux assumed the man was about to order. The entire room waited in anticipation while Tong's and Child's fingers continued to tap away at their tasks. Morrison finally spoke, delivering two words that might prevent a greater war, or cause an international incident.

"Do it."

Skeleton Lake

Uttarakhand, India

"You want to do what?" Jack stared incredulously at Acton as gunfire continued from three positions, the Chinese now holding back behind their armored Mercedes.

"We need to blow the entrance."

"You do realize that traps us inside, which sort of accomplishes their goal."

"There are supplies inside and enough air to last a small number of people days, if not weeks."

"But how do we get out?"

"They can dig us out."

"Who?"

"The Indians, whoever the hell is sent to rescue us. Laura's got the satphone." He twisted around. "Laura, bring the satphone!"

"Coming!"

"We call, tell them where we are, blow the entrance. The Chinese aren't going to bother trying to dig us out. We'll just wait for things to settle down."

Jack glanced at Kumar. "What do you think, Captain?"

"I think it's the dumbest plan I've ever heard. Unfortunately, I can't think of a better one. We can't hold them off here much longer, we're going to run out of ammo eventually, Chinese reinforcements are going to arrive, or there's going to be a missile strike. None of those end up good for us."

Laura cursed behind them and Acton spun. "What's wrong?"

She emerged from the dark, holding up the satellite phone, a hole in the casing. "It looks like it caught a bullet. It must have been at the roadblock."

Acton cursed. "Cellphones?"

"There's no coverage in this area," replied Kumar.

"What about your comms?" asked Jack.

"Still down."

Acton pointed at the SAM battery. "What about theirs?"

"They use the same equipment we do. They should be down as well."

"We need to confirm that," said Jack. "Your comms could be silent for an entirely different reason, technical or operational."

Major Singh shouted something and his entire team sprinted away from the SAM battery. Acton cursed as he stared at the pile of loose stone that had fallen just from the rumbling of the treads of the mobile unit. The detonation of an incoming missile could bring down half the mountain.

"The decision's been made for us. Get inside, now!" He turned and grabbed Laura, sprinting deeper into the cave. He glanced over his shoulder to see Jack following after a moment's hesitation. Kumar and his men remained behind, firing at the Chinese and beckoning for Singh's men to come toward the cave. As Acton rounded a bend in the tunnel and emerged into the large chamber, a massive eruption behind them shook the mountain. Stalactites, formed over centuries and millennia, broke free from above, crashing onto the hard surface below.

He pointed at an alcove. "Everybody in there!"

Reading hustled Tommy and Mai into the natural shelter as Laura, Acton, and Jack followed, but by the time they were all squeezed in, the rumbling had stopped. Acton tentatively poked his head out, staring up at the roof of the cave. "I think we're okay, but be careful, some may just be hanging on by a thread. Stick close to the walls."

"I think I'm going to stick right here," said Mai. Tommy eagerly agreed.

Acton patted them both on the shoulder. "Good thinking." He turned to Jack. "I'm going to check on the captain."

"I'm coming with you."

"Me too," said Reading.

Jack led the way in the dim light still cast by several of the battery-powered lights left behind by Jagmeet Sharma's team. Acton pointed at them. "We're going to want to conserve those. Let's turn them all off except for one."

Laura nodded. "I'm on it."

Acton pulled out his cellphone and turned on the flashlight, leading the way through the narrow passage, finding a large pile of stone where the entrance once was.

Jack stood, his hands on his hips, shaking his head. "Well, Doc, looks like your plan worked."

"Not for everyone." Reading stepped closer then his hand suddenly darted out. "Help me!"

Acton gasped as an arm was revealed. He and Jack both rushed in, yanking stones out of the way as Reading continued to pull. It didn't take long and they had Kumar on the cave floor. Jack leaned over him and checked for a pulse. "He's not breathing." He immediately began CPR.

Reading turned around. "Medic!"

Footfalls echoed and within moments, Raj's medic took over the chest compressions. Suddenly Kumar gasped and bolted upright. He coughed several times and spat out a mix of dirt and bile as his medic checked him over.

"We need to dig this out," said Reading. "See if we can get to the others."

Jack stared at the pile of stone. "This is pretty unstable. By the time we could safely get to them they'll be dead, and we might just kill ourselves in the process."

Kumar pushed to his feet and shook his head. "They were too far out when the Chinese missile hit. They were trying to provide cover fire for the SAM crew to get into the cave. They would've all been caught in the explosion."

Reading closed his eyes for a moment. "Let's just hope those bloody Chinese got caught in it as well."

Kumar brushed off. "Unfortunately, they were probably far enough away to survive."

"So, what you're telling us is that the only people on this planet who know where we are, are the Chinese who are trying to kill us?"

Kumar chuckled. "That about sums it up."

"So now what do we do?"

"Follow my plan," replied Acton.

"And just what is that?"

"We wait."

Indian Airspace

West of Udhampur, India

Dawson pressed his finger against his earpiece. "Repeat that, Control."

"Zero-One, this is Control Actual."

Dawson frowned. What had sounded like a garbled order was about to be confirmed by Leroux, which suggested he had heard the orders correctly the first time.

"We believe Colonel Mandal is somehow involved in today's events. We need his cellphone. Do you have eyes on him?"

"We had eyes on him a few minutes ago, sir. He was getting in what appeared to be a civilian vehicle just before the Chinese attack."

"You need to find him, Zero-One. Try to take him alive and get his cellphone. It could have the proof that not only is he behind the death of Senator Simmons, but is also somehow involved with the Chinese. That cellphone could be the key to ending this war."

"Roger that, Control, we're on it. If you've got satellite coverage of the area, it was a black late-model SUV parked on the road running in front of the headquarters' main entrance, and it didn't pull away until about ninety seconds before the initial impact."

"Copy that, Zero-One, we'll try to find something, but satellite capabilities are just coming back online after the Chinese launched their anti-satellite missiles and scrambled the heavens for God knows how long."

"Copy that, Control. We'll do our best."

"Good hunting, Zero-One. Control, out."

Dawson turned to the others. "Eyeballs on the ground, gentlemen. We're looking for the black SUV the colonel got in." He headed to the cockpit. "We need to turn back."

Estevez twisted in his seat. "I had heard Army boys are dumb, but I guess I didn't realize how dumb. Why the hell would you want to head back to a heap of rubble?"

"Because the man possibly responsible for this entire war is getting away. He's in a black SUV that left the headquarters just before the first missile struck. We need to find him and get his cellphone. We might be able to stop this war."

"Good enough for me." Estevez banked them hard to the right, pulling a 180 as Dawson gripped a handhold until they leveled out again.

"Hopefully, we'll have some satellite intel to let us know where he went, then we might get to see what this bird can actually do in action."

"I think you'll be impressed, Sergeant Major. She's a capable gal, despite what you might read on the bathroom wall."

Dawson chuckled. "I have no doubt. Let me know when we get back in the vicinity. I'm going to brief my men."

"Will do, Sergeant Major."

Dawson headed back to the cabin, everyone still staring out the windows.

"What's up, BD?" asked Niner. "Why are we searching for the colonel?"

"Because Control believes he might be involved in the assassination of Senator Simmons and somehow involved in triggering this war. They think the proof is on his cellphone. If we can get our hands on it, and get our hands on him, preferably alive, then we might be able to stop this thing before it turns into a complete Charlie-Foxtrot." He turned to Captain Patel. "Sir, I realize we're operating on Indian soil. Any assistance you can provide would be appreciated."

Patel stared at him. "The very idea that Colonel Mandal would be behind this is laughable. He's the most loyal soldier I know. He would never betray his country like this."

"Sir, I'm not aware of the particulars, however I know the source. If those people think he's involved, he's involved. My orders are to capture the man alive, if possible, and take possession of the cellphone that could prove not only his guilt but also his innocence. This operation would go a whole lot easier if you were behind it, sir."

Patel regarded him for a moment. "Do you agree to operate under my command?"

"No." Dawson smiled slightly. "Though I will agree to *pretend* to operate under your command."

Patel chuckled. "I like the way you think, Sergeant Major. We'll find the colonel and examine his cellphone, and when we prove his innocence, I think you'll be buying the beer."

Dawson bowed his head slightly. "Sounds reasonable. And if I'm right?"

Patel sighed. "Then I fear there'll be nothing to celebrate."

Skeleton Lake

Uttarakhand, India

Acton headed back to the chamber with the others. Tommy rose. "What was that?"

"Some sort of air-to-ground missile," said Jack. "They took out the SAM site. And to answer your next question, yes, the cave entrance is blocked."

Mai stepped closer to Tommy and he put his arm around her. "Did you get the call out in time?" she asked Laura.

Laura held up the damaged phone. "No."

Tommy cursed and stepped forward, taking the phone. "I wish I had my toolkit with me."

Jack reached into his pocket and pulled out a Swiss Army knife, tossing it to him. "There might be some things on there that can help you out, but don't you dare use my toothpick. That's just gross."

Tommy began opening every attachment to see what was available as he slowly drifted back to the alcove with Mai. Acton faced the large

258

chamber and assessed the situation. He pointed at a stack of supplies that Sharma's team had moved in for just such a situation. "Let's inventory what we've got. Jagmeet said he brought in supplies that would last his team several days."

"How long do you think we're going to have to last in here?" asked Laura.

Acton shook his head. "I have no idea." He turned to Kumar. "Sir, how long before your people will come searching for you?"

"Not until things settle down. Once they reestablish communications and we don't respond, we'll likely be added to a long list of missing, presumed dead. And even if they did start searching, we're nowhere near our last reported position. There's no way in hell they're going to find us in here."

"What about the SAM site?" asked Reading. "Surely somebody will come to investigate that."

"That's our only hope. Eventually they will come to check on those men, but that'll be a recovery operation, and it won't begin until the Chinese are out of this area."

Laura squeezed Acton's hand. "You mean when the war is over."

"Not only when the war is over, but when my side has won, which wasn't looking too promising the last time I checked. I'd say we'll be in here for days, perhaps weeks, and even if we did win the war tomorrow and my people did come into this area, would they even think to check this cave? Does anybody even know about it?"

Acton shook his head. "Besides us, only Jagmeet's team knows, and I doubt he'd be coming back into this area until peace has been restored."

Reading tilted his head back. "So, in other words, we're bollocksed."

Jack held up a finger. "You're forgetting one thing."

"What's that?"

"You've got me."

Acton eyed him. "Unless you're going to tell me you've got some sort of James Bond laser that'll slice through the rocks, I'm not sure how you being here helps us."

"Well, let me explain just how lucky you are. I am a *critical* United States government asset whose training cost millions. They *will* be searching for me."

Acton tilted to the side and checked Jack's ass. Jack turned to give him a better look.

"Like what you see?"

Acton frowned. "Not particularly. I don't see some high-tech transmitter shoved up there."

Jack chuckled. "You're forgetting, nobody has more eyes in the sky than Uncle Sam. I can guarantee you, they had eyes on us the entire time. They know where we drove to. I wouldn't be surprised if they already have an extraction team headed our way."

"You seem rather confident," said Reading.

"That's because I have an extremely high opinion of myself and truly do believe that America can't afford to lose someone as great as I am."

Kumar cocked an eyebrow and glanced at Acton. "Is this guy for real?"

Acton shrugged. "I never really know. I have another friend who does the same job and he's just as cocky, so maybe it's a prerequisite for getting hired."

"Well, regardless of his high opinion of himself, he is right about one thing. No one has more eyes in the sky than America. If we have any hope of getting rescued, it'll be by his people." He pointed at the supplies. "In the meantime, however, we need to stretch this out as long as we can. It could take weeks."

Acton frowned. "I'm afraid, Captain, that unless there's another way for fresh air to get in here other than that collapsed entrance, we'll have run out of air long before these supplies."

Operations Center 2, CIA Headquarters

Langley, Virginia

"Any sign of them?"

Tong shook her head. "Not yet. I followed the road they were on for as far as they could've gone in the time we were blacked out, but nothing."

Leroux frowned. "Then they must've turned off the main road."

Tong agreed. "They were probably trying to avoid more roadblocks."

"They're probably trying to hide somewhere they won't be spotted by the Chinese."

Tong ran her fingers through her hair. "Do you think they'd try to hide the vehicle itself?"

Leroux pursed his lips then sighed. "These are smart people with more combat experience than you or I. And if I were them, I'd be finding some out-of-the-way place, then covering my vehicle with tree branches or brush or whatever I could find so that it couldn't be spotted from the air."

Tong cursed. "Well, that just made my job a hell of a lot more difficult."

Leroux patted her on the back. "I have faith in you, and I'm sure the Chief won't be too angry if you can't find them before the Chinese do. After all, he only said it was his fault they were there."

She stared up at him. "You're not helping."

He laughed and headed back to his station. "I'm sorry, I couldn't resist. Just keep doing what you're doing. You'll find them, I'm sure."

Child spun in his chair, a victory finger in the air. "Speaking of finding people, I think I found our missing colonel."

"Where?"

The victory finger bent toward the display and Leroux turned to see a satellite image showing a shot of a collection of vehicles, primarily military.

"Where is this?"

"It looks like some sort of warehouse, about five miles from the headquarters. The perimeter security, though, makes me think it's not industrial, it's actually a military complex."

Leroux watched the live feed showing military vehicles lined up, entering the building through a set of large garage doors, including a black SUV that matched the description of the colonel's vehicle. "Is that him?"

"Yeah, I managed to get a shot of his tags and matched it to a shot we had of the HQ before we lost coverage. It's the vehicle he escaped in, all right, but whether he's inside it, I don't know."

Tong turned in her chair. "If he's trying to escape, why would he go there? If there's any place he's going to get caught, it's going to be on government property."

Leroux fit his headgear in place. "You're forgetting he was escaping the Chinese missiles. As far as he knows, we're not on to him, he's getting away with it. If he were to go anywhere else but this backup command center, it would raise suspicions." He activated his comms. "Bravo Zero-One, this is Control Actual, do you read, over?"

"Copy that, Control. I read you, over."

"Zero-One, we've got a position for you. Transmitting the coordinates to you and your pilot now." He indicated with a wave of his finger for Child to send the coordinates. "It looks like a secondary command location, about five miles north of Northern Command Headquarters. We're going to send you a satellite shot now showing the area." Another wave of a finger.

"Done," reported Child.

"Control, this is Osprey Two-Niner, confirming coordinates received. What are your orders, over?"

"Osprey Two-Niner, Control. Proceed to those coordinates and land at your discretion. We believe you'll be received as friendlies, however, expect that status to change after Bravo Team proceeds with their mission, over."

"Understood, Control. We've saved their asses once already today, why not twice? Two-Niner, out."

Dawson cut in. "I've got the satellite imagery. Keep us updated if anything changes. Hopefully the Indians will be just as curious to find out the truth as we are. Captain Patel certainly is."

"Good luck, Zero-One. We'll be monitoring. Control, out." Leroux sighed and removed his headset. "We might just get out of this yet."

Approaching Udhampur, India

Dawson poked his head in the cockpit. "ETA?"

Estevez glanced over his shoulder at him. "Three minutes. Instructions?"

Dawson held out the tablet showing the overhead shot. He pointed at a large, paved area in front of the building. "I say we just land there. We're friendlies, we land, we disembark, we do our business, we leave."

"And should this business go south?"

"We leave in a hurry, so keep things powered up."

Estevez rolled his eyes. "Will do, but remember, we don't exactly leave like a bat out of hell in this beast."

"If we're leaving in a hurry, we probably have their colonel, so they might not be too eager to fire on the aircraft."

"There's that famous word, 'might.'"

Dawson shrugged. "I'm not too worried about it."

Estevez eyed him. "And why is that?"

"Because the moment my foot hits that ramp, anything that happens after is your fault."

Estevez flipped him the bird. "Get the hell out of my cockpit, Sergeant Major."

Dawson grinned. "Aye aye, sir." He returned to the cabin where the others were checking their gear. "Now remember, Captain Patel leads the way. We follow, patrol carry—we don't want anybody panicking. We're just friendly Americans arriving to lend a hand. When we confront the colonel, I suspect it'll go one of two ways. He'll calmly surrender, or he'll try to turn his men on us. And remember, we don't know who's working with him. All it takes is one or two to turn this into a Charlie-Foxtrot."

Niner leaned forward. "And if things go south?"

"Grab the colonel, use him as a human shield, fall back using the vehicles as cover, get on board the aircraft, then hope the Indians aren't going to try to shoot us down with the colonel on board. Questions?"

"What's more important, him or his cellphone?" asked Atlas.

"His cellphone. Whatever happens, we leave there with the phone first, him second. Langley believes that what's on that phone could prove the reasons behind this war are bullshit."

"Sixty seconds," reported Estevez over the speakers.

"This is it, gentleman, let's try to keep casualties to a minimum."

"Always sound advice," commented Niner.

Atlas punched him on the shoulder, sending him stumbling. "He's not talking about us, knucklehead. He's talking about the Indians."

"Oh, that makes more sense, though it kind of hurts my feelings that BD doesn't think we should keep *our* casualties down."

Patel gave Dawson a look. "How do you put up with it, Sergeant Major?"

Dawson chuckled. "I have a woman at home who loves me and has met him, so she knows exactly what I'm going through."

Patel laughed. "Then you're a lucky man. My wife has never met any of those who aggravate me. Perhaps if she did, she might understand me a little better."

The attitude of the plane changed as the rotors tilted upward. Dawson hit the button for the ramp and it lowered as the Osprey bounced to a textbook landing, its ass-end facing the gaggle of vehicles. Patel led the way and the rest of them followed, Dawson at Patel's right shoulder.

Patel pointed. "There's Colonel Mandal."

Dawson spotted Mandal surrounded by at least half a dozen of his men. He was giving orders as if nothing were out of the ordinary. There was no hint the man knew what was about to happen, and it had Dawson wondering if Langley were right, though his doubts weren't about to have him ignoring his orders. Risking embarrassment wasn't a concern when a murderer and traitor could potentially be captured.

Patel's pace quickened slightly, the man's nerves getting to him.

"Easy, Captain. We're all friends here, remember?"

Patel slowed up and Mandal spotted them, a smile spreading. "Captain! Sergeant Major! I'm relieved to see you made it out alive." Patel stopped and saluted, Mandal returning it. "Captain, now that you're here, I want you to coordinate—"

Patel cut him off. "Colonel, I must speak with you in private."

Mandal dismissed those around them with a flick of the wrist, leaving them alone. Dawson's men casually repositioned to surround the colonel and observe the soldiers in the immediate vicinity. Dawson quickly assessed every man around them, most going about their business off-loading supplies and reinforcing a security perimeter, few paying attention to their arrival.

"What is it, Captain? I'm busy here."

"Yes, Colonel. Information has come to light through the Americans, and I'm almost embarrassed to ask, Colonel, but I need to ask you for your cellphone."

Dawson's eyes, hidden behind his ballistic glasses, noted the colonel's nostrils flare and his shoulders square slightly. "Captain?"

"Sir, if you would just give me your cellphone, we can clear this up immediately. I've assured them that there's nothing to find, that this is all a misunderstanding, and it can all be cleared up just by showing them your cellphone."

Mandal's chest swelled and he directed his glare at Dawson. "Sergeant Major, perhaps you better explain what's going on here. My captain's being far too diplomatic."

Dawson gave a curt nod and delivered the dirt. Straight. "Of course, Colonel. We have reason to believe you were involved in the murder of Senator Simmons and have been providing intel to the Chinese, who warned you of the missile attack on your headquarters so that you could escape in time."

This had everybody within earshot stopping, for Dawson had made sure he said it loudly enough for all to hear. This was the moment of truth. How would these troops react? Would they want to defend their commander, not believing the accusations, or would they be so appalled at the possibility of them being true, that they would not interfere?

"Are you accusing me of being a traitor, Sergeant Major?"

"Sir, at the moment, I'm accusing your phone of being a traitor. I don't care about you. My orders are to seize your phone so that we can see what's on it. Hand it over now, and we can end this very quickly. Don't hand it over…well, sir, I think you know what could happen."

"I know what could happen, Sergeant Major, but I get the sense that you don't." Mandal took a step back. "Arrest these men!"

His soldiers stood startled, uncertain as to what to do. Captain Patel, however, reacted immediately. "Belay that order! Arrest the colonel!"

Weapons were raised all around them, one of the men aiming his directly at Patel's chest. "Sorry, Captain, I'm not in your chain of command, but I am in his. Arrest the captain and the Americans!"

Dawson stepped forward and grabbed Mandal by the shirt, yanking him closer and twisting him around. He pressed his Glock against Mandal's temple. "Now, everybody's going to remain calm," he said as he slowly backed toward the Osprey, its engines powering up from idle as Estevez was obviously paying attention to the proceedings. "Nobody does anything stupid and the colonel lives. All we want is his phone."

Patel backed away with Dawson and the others. "Ask yourselves this. If he's innocent, why won't he just hand his phone over?"

"Colonel, what should we do?" asked his lone vocal supporter.

"Kill them all!"

Dawson pressed the muzzle of his weapon harder against Mandal's skull. "The first shot I hear fired, I squeeze the trigger, your colonel is dead. My men are wearing full body armor and they're American Special Forces. You may take us out, but not before we take out ten times as many of you, all to protect a man who might be a traitor who started this war. Stand down, and nobody dies here, and maybe we end a war."

"You have your orders!" shouted Mandal, and it was evident to Dawson the man had a death wish. The soldier causing problems raised his weapon and Dawson quickly put two in his chest before pressing the muzzle back against Mandal's skull. Dawson continued to back away toward the Osprey, using the vehicles as cover for their right flank.

"Everybody just remain calm," said Patel, his hands extended in front of him, palms up. "Nobody else has to die. All we want is the truth."

"Sniper on the roof," warned Niner.

Dawson's eyes darted up and he spotted the target readying his weapon. "Take him out."

Niner's M4 belched lead, three well-aimed rapid shots eliminating the threat. They continued to back out, but the tension levels were rising. Any moment now, a nervous trigger finger could turn this into a bloodbath. These were innocent soldiers just doing their job, and he could just imagine what he'd be thinking if a group of Indian soldiers showed up on Fort Bragg and attempted to arrest Colonel Clancy at gunpoint. He'd be killing those Indians without hesitation before asking questions.

Atlas spotted him first, a soldier to their left, sweating profusely, his eyes wide with fear and panic, the veins on his neck popping as his hands gripping his rifle shook. He swung the barrel of his weapon toward them and Atlas fired two rounds into the man's chest.

Things were about to go Antarctic South.

"Into the cars!" Dawson dragged Mandal with him as he ducked between a troop transport and a jeep. The others did the same as gunfire erupted all around them. Dawson took a knee but kept the colonel standing, the gun now pressed against the base of the man's spine. His comms crackled in his ear.

"Zero-One, Control. What's your status, over?"

"Our status is we're going to be cut apart unless we start fighting back, over."

"Do you have the colonel's phone?"

"Stand by, Control." Dawson patted down the man's pockets, finding it in his front right. He pulled out the phone. "I've got it."

"Get him to log in."

Dawson yanked the man down to the ground, gripping his skull tightly as he held the phone up to Mandal's face. The device unlocked and he shoved the colonel back to his feet, jamming his weapon back into the man's spine. "I'm in."

"Copy that, Zero-One. Stand by." Dawson glanced down at the phone and saw a download begin then complete a few moments later. "We're in, Zero-One. Make sure nothing happens to that phone while we download the data. We'll also need it for evidence."

"Well, if you find anything on this, don't keep it to yourselves. Share it with whoever the hell's in charge here right now. Maybe they can get them to stand down."

"Copy that, Zero-One. Will do. Control, out."

Shouts erupted from the warehouse entrance and Dawson poked his head up to see a dozen well-armed, well-equipped men wearing spec ops gear racing into the fray. He cursed at the arrival of a real challenge, but was surprised to hear them ordering their comrades to cease fire. The gunfire dwindled, but didn't stop, not everyone hearing the order.

Mandal stared down at him, sneering. "You're dead now, Sergeant Major. You and your men are dead."

Dawson pressed the barrel of his Glock harder against the base of the man's spine. "I'm not going to kill you, Colonel. I'm just going to make sure you never walk again so that you can suffer for the rest of your life."

"I can live with that, Sergeant Major."

Dawson surreptitiously activated his comms so everyone could hear what was being said. "Colonel, my mission's already been accomplished. The data's being downloaded from your phone as we speak, and your actions here today have proven your guilt. If what my people believe is true, we'll have helped stop this war, and if the six of us dying saves thousands of lives, I can go to my grave comfortably with that knowledge. The question is, Colonel, when I give the order to fight back, how many of your men am I taking with me, all because they unknowingly protected a traitor?"

"I'm no traitor. I'm a patriot. I did what was necessary to save my country."

"By selling it out to the Chinese?" Dawson spotted the Special Forces team spreading out exactly as he would have his own men do.

Leroux whispered in his ear. "Zero-One, Control. We found the proof. It was on his phone. He was sending false intel to the Chinese, making it look like the communications facility was being constructed to accelerate a build-up in the area with the ultimate goal of taking back and holding the disputed zone."

Dawson didn't respond to Leroux's update, but continued working Mandal. "You fed false intel to the Chinese, making them think that India was going to attack them first so you could trigger a war. How many hundreds have died already? How many thousands? Why did you do it, Colonel? Why did you betray your country?"

"I didn't betray my country, I saved my country. I showed the threat the Chinese posed to us. I've shown those morons in New Delhi that China can't be trusted, that we have to take a stronger stand, and by making it look like the Kashmiris were behind this, we could deal with the other problem that we face. Separatists within our borders can't be tolerated."

"So then, you're admitting to everything? That it was your man that murdered the senator, that you fed false intel to the Chinese in order to trigger this war, and framed the Kashmiris so you could initiate a crackdown?"

"Of course I admit it. I'm proud of what I've done and I'll be hailed a hero because of it. But, Sergeant Major, my confession has only been heard by a dead man. Once I give the order, my team, who are completely loyal to me, will take out every one of your men. What does it feel like to know that everyone under your command has less than thirty seconds to live?"

"I think you underestimate your men, Colonel." He tapped his earpiece and Mandal's eyes flared. "Control, did you get all that?"

"Affirmative, Zero-One."

"We need to be able to rebroadcast it so these people can hear what was said."

"On your six!" hissed Niner. Dawson didn't bother confirming it was his comrade, instead racking his brain for a way everyone could hear the confession.

"Try this," said Niner as he arrived at a crouch, the gunfire now halted, though for how long, who knew. "I found it on the seat of an MP vehicle."

Dawson looked to see Niner holding out a megaphone. "Perfect. Turn it on, make sure it works."

Niner flicked a switch and there was a squawk before he placed it to his lips. "Testing one—"

Dawson cut him off with a raised hand. "It works. Control, we've got a megaphone here. Call my phone and I'll put it on speaker—"

"Way ahead of you, Zero-One."

His phone vibrated in his pocket and Dawson took a knee, tilting his head toward it. "Get it. Front right."

Niner reached in. "Ooh, Maggie's a lucky girl."

"Do you really think this is the time?"

275

Niner withdrew the vibrating phone. "It's always the time." He swiped to take the call. "Zero-One's phone, who may I ask is calling?"

Dawson rolled his eyes then slowly rose, repositioning his weapon against Mandal's temple. He spotted the soldier giving the orders thirty yards out.

"Are you ready to surrender, or do I order my men to engage?"

Dawson bowed his head slightly to the man. "Major, there's something you need to hear."

The megaphone squawked once again and Niner replayed the conversation, and as the colonel's confession was revealed, eyes widened and jaws dropped. When the recording was finished playing, Dawson lowered his weapon.

"All the proof is on his phone. We've transmitted all the data to our people and they've confirmed everything that was said. He fed the Chinese false intel to trigger this war." He holstered his weapon and held out his hand for Niner, who placed the phone in it. Dawson raised it. "Right here, sir. All the proof that everything happening here today shouldn't be. Now, I'm willing to order my men to stand down if you're willing to order yours to do the same. No one else has to die here today, and the sooner we get this proof into the hands of our respective governments, the sooner a dialogue can open up, and perhaps we can stop this war before things really get out of control."

The Indian major lowered his weapon. "Everybody, stand down. The first man that shoots, I kill him personally."

Dawson watched as weapons lowered, and when enough were no longer pointing in his team's direction, he gave the order. "Stand down,

Bravo Team." Heads poked up from the cluster of vehicles surrounding him. He cautiously led the colonel out as the major approached with two of his men.

"Major, I want you to arrest the Americans! That's an order!" barked Mandal, but the major ignored him.

"I'm Major Devi."

Dawson snapped to attention and saluted the man, as did the rest of his team. The salute was returned. "I'm Sergeant Major White, sir."

"We'll take custody of the prisoner now."

Dawson pushed Mandal forward and the two men accompanying Devi each took the disgraced colonel by the arm.

"Colonel Mandal, I'm placing you under arrest for suspicion of treason and murder." Devi jerked a thumb over his shoulder. "Search him and lock him up. Nobody speaks to him."

"Yes, sir," replied the men.

Mandal was led away, and to his credit, he remained silent, maintaining what little dignity he had left. Devi turned to the scores of nervous soldiers still surrounding them. "Everyone sling your weapons and get back to work. We've still got a war to fight."

Nobody moved, everyone staring at each other, uncertain as to what to do.

"Now, people! That's an order!"

Someone moved, then another, and within moments, the bustle of activity that had preceded their arrival resumed. Dawson turned and gave a thumbs-up to Estevez and the massive rotors powered back down to idle. He held up a finger to Devi. "Control, Zero-One. I assume you're still monitoring. Situation is under control, over."

"Copy that, Zero-One. The evidence you collected is being transmitted now."

"Control, what do you want us to do with the phone?"

Devi raised a hand, answering the question. "I think until we know who's loyal to whom, you should keep that."

"Thank you, Major. Control, Zero-One, the Indian major in command of the scene has indicated we can maintain possession of the phone for security purposes."

"Copy that, Zero-One." Something was shouted in the background. "Stand by, Zero-One." Leroux cursed. "Zero-One, you have missiles inbound. I repeat, you have missiles inbound. Evacuate immediately, over."

"Copy that, Control." Dawson spun his hand over his head, signaling Estevez to power up. "Major, we've got missiles inbound. Evacuate your people immediately." He jerked his thumb at the Osprey. "I've got room for about twenty more."

Devi spun on his heel, spotting his two men with the colonel. "Get the colonel on the plane!" he shouted. The two men turned. "On the plane! Missiles are inbound! Everyone evac now!" He turned to Dawson. "Not that I want to save the man's life, but we may need his testimony to stop this war."

"Good thinking, Major."

An alarm sounded and Dawson and his team sprinted toward the lowered ramp of the Osprey, its rotors now fully powered up, ready to take off. The two soldiers hauled Mandal on board and Devi remained on the concrete.

"Major, we have room for you and your men."

Devi shook his head. "Negative, Sergeant Major, our place is here."

Niner and the others were ushering some of the Indians on board. "We're full up, BD," said Niner as he stepped onto the ramp.

Dawson saluted the major. "Good luck, sir."

Devi returned it. "Thank you, Sergeant Major."

Dawson stepped inside and hit the button to the ramp and it slowly raised as he headed deeper inside. "Let's go!" The Osprey's engines whined and she lifted off the ground, once again with missiles inbound. "Control, Zero-One, ETA on those inbounds?"

"Three minutes. I repeat, three minutes. Are you clear?"

"We will be," replied Dawson. He faced the cabin and found everyone strapping in, his men helping those too panicked to buckle up properly. He dropped into a free seat and buckled in as the Osprey's rotors tilted forward and they put some distance between the impending target and themselves. He peered down at the scene below, the tangle of vehicles that had escaped from the primary headquarters now a bottleneck that couldn't be cleared in time. Vehicles were abandoned as hundreds of people sprinted toward the fences. He spotted Major Devi and his men heroically directing people, Captain Patel at their side.

But they were too late.

The first missile slammed directly into the compound, the facility never designed for such an attack. The walls blew out, sending shards of metal and debris in all directions, cutting down those within its reach.

The second detonated and Dawson closed his eyes, for it had missed the building and landed directly in the parking lot, incinerating everyone in sight. He turned back to face the cabin, his eyes burning, his chest tight. Everyone was subdued, some of the soldiers they had rescued sobbing from the horrors of what they had just seen, and from the guilt they felt for having survived what their comrades hadn't.

It was a feeling he knew well, and it was a feeling they would never forget.

Skeleton Lake

Uttarakhand, India

Reading and Jack emerged from the tunnel filthy and exhausted. They both sat, their shoulders sagging, their arms dangling. Mai brought them both water that they drained quickly.

"Any progress?" asked Acton.

Reading shrugged. "Who the hell knows? We pulled out tons of rock, but every time I think we're getting close there's another cave-in. We could be one meter from freedom, or twenty. I have no idea."

"Well, all we can do is keep trying. If we don't get through, we're going to suffocate."

Tommy looked up from the satellite phone he had been working on for the past two days in the hopes he could get it to connect to the satellite network so their friends stateside might trace it. But beyond a few minutes of life, he had had little success. "Do you feel that?"

"Feel what?" asked Laura.

"The ground's vibrating again."

Reading cursed as he pushed to his feet. "Lovely."

Acton stretched out his arms, herding everyone toward the walls. "Everybody take cover. Watch your heads."

The vibrations turned into an audible rumble as everyone squeezed into various alcoves scouted out since they were trapped here, stalagmites still occasionally dropping from the missile explosion that had taken out the SAM site.

"Is it another rockslide?" asked Jack, huddled with Reading nearby.

Acton shook his head. "I don't know." He pressed his hand against the rock, the vibrations pulsing his arm. "It feels almost rhythmic." The pulsations slowed as the rumble waned and slowly came to a stop. He tentatively emerged from his cover, eying the ceiling warily.

"What do you think that was?" asked Laura.

Kumar was the first to speculate. "I think it might have been a helicopter."

Mai's face brightened. "You mean we're saved?"

Jack shook his head. "Don't get your hopes up. They could be here to check on that SAM site and have no clue we're even in here."

"I'm going to go check to see if I hear anything." Acton headed down the tunnel toward the blocked entrance, everyone eagerly following. He approached the rock pile and leaned close. "Hello! Is anyone out there?" There was no reply. There could be twenty feet of debris between them and any ears.

Tommy held up a rock. "Try Morse Code."

Acton smiled and took it, then tapped out an SOS, careful not to disturb the rock too much.

Reading growled and picked up his own. "Love taps aren't going to be heard. Everybody stand back." He smacked hard three times, then three times slower, then three times fast again before pausing. Nothing. He repeated it then paused.

Acton threw up his hands in excitement as they heard three faint raps in reply. A series of taps followed.

"What are they saying?" asked Laura.

The old school soldier, Reading, translated. "They're saying, 'Stand back.'"

"Holy shit, they're not going to blow it, are they?" asked Tommy, scrambling away from the pile of rock.

"Let's hope they're smarter than that," said Acton as everyone rushed back down the tunnel and into the chamber. "Let's take cover, just in case."

Reading emerged, having sent the acknowledgment, and more vibrations trembled through the cave. "All right, everybody. Let's take cover. Watch your heads because I have no idea what they're planning out there." Vibrations mixed with jolts, the pattern alternating repeatedly, and everyone exchanged curious glances.

"What do you think that is?" asked Laura.

Acton shrugged. "No idea, but it feels like some sort of engine gearing up and gearing down."

"Some sort of front loader?" suggested Tommy. "Those jolts could be the scoop when it hits stone."

Acton's head bobbed. "As good a guess as any. If that's the case, they could have us out of here pretty quick."

Reading grunted. "Assuming the mountain doesn't come down on top of them too."

Jack eyed him. "You're just always the pessimist, aren't you?"

Reading glared. "I'm supposed to be on a beach in Spain tanning my white ass, worrying about sand getting up my crack, but instead I'm here seeing the sights in India." He shot a particular stink eye at Acton and Laura.

"Sorry," said Laura meekly. "Still love me?"

"Of course." Reading jerked his chin at Acton. "Him, I'm not so sure about."

Acton sighed. "I always knew she was your favorite."

"Wait!" Tommy held up a finger. "It stopped!"

A breeze hit Acton's face. "Do you feel that?" He sniffed. "It's fresh air!"

"Hello, anybody home?"

Acton sprang to his feet with a broad smile, recognizing the voice. Laura leaped up beside him. "Is that you, Niner?"

"You got it, sweetheart. Just remember who saved you. It was me, not that girly-man of a husband."

"Who's calling who a girly-man?" rumbled Atlas, his voice so deep, Acton for a moment feared he might trigger another collapse. They headed into the tunnel and rounded the corner of the final bend, sunlight revealing a significant chunk of the entrance cleared.

"Let's get everyone out of there fast," came Dawson's voice. "We don't know how long this is going to hold."

"We've got a wounded man," said Kumar.

"Please identify yourself."

"I'm Captain Kumar, Indian Army."

"Sergeant Major White, United States Army. We've got people out here who'll be happy to hear you're alive, sir."

Acton urged Mai toward the entrance. "Ladies first."

Mai's eyes bulged. "If you think I'm going through first, you don't know me at all."

Acton chuckled and Laura stepped into the opening. "I'll go first." She gingerly picked her way through then Mai followed with Tommy. Raj arrived with the medic and they were helped out by Kumar.

Acton held out a hand toward the exit, smiling at Reading. "Age before beauty."

Reading growled, muttering some combination of bollocks and bloody hell this or that. He disappeared through the opening then Acton turned to Jack. "Be my guest."

Jack shook his head. "Sorry, Doc, you already said it, age before beauty."

Acton groaned.

"Doesn't feel so good when you're on the other end of it, does it?"

Acton climbed through the hole. "No, it doesn't."

He emerged on the other side to sunlight. Jack followed a moment later as Acton shook the hands of the Bravo Team members near the entrance. "You have no idea how happy I am to see you guys."

Niner waved a hand in front of his nose, squinting. "So were we, Doc, until we got a whiff of you. My God, I don't know if I want to let you on the bird. They'll be hosing that thing down for a week just to get rid of the smell."

"Is that everyone?" asked Dawson.

Jack nodded. "Yeah, I was the last one out."

"Then let's get away from this damn cliff face. I don't trust it." Dawson led them away from the danger area as the front loader that had freed them powered up and drove back toward the road leading into the valley, which was when Acton noticed an Osprey sitting where the cars had been parked when this entire fiasco began. Dawson twirled his hand in the air and the unique aircraft powered up. Kumar and his men were talking with a group of Indian soldiers near a troop transport, and Acton made to say goodbye when Dawson stopped him.

"You'll see them where we're heading, Doc. Right now, let's just get you to safety. There's a lot of people worried about you."

"How did you find us?"

Dawson pointed up. "Eyes in the sky, Doc. It took them a while, but they found where you went. Then it was just a matter of waiting for the Chinese to pull out of the area."

Acton glanced up at the sky as several planes roared overhead. "The war?"

"It's over."

Reading's eyebrow shot up. "Really? So soon?"

"There was more going on than you're probably aware of."

"Ooh, do tell?" said Jack. "I do love a good story."

"I'll fill you in on the ride, but first we need to get everyone to safety. Everyone is horny to get you all back stateside."

"Who's 'everyone?'" asked Acton. "I owe someone a punch in the nose."

Dawson chuckled. "I think I might know who that someone is, but just know he's why we were sent into the area, and why Jack had your back."

"So, what? I'm supposed to thank him?"

"I say you call it even, and if you ever meet him face-to-face, you leave his nose alone."

Acton grunted. "Perhaps. We'll see how I'm feeling that day."

They boarded the Osprey and Acton strapped in beside Laura and the others, one side of the aircraft filled with their friends from Bravo Team, the other with a group of filthy civilians who indeed did stink. Laura rested her head on his shoulder and he gently kissed her forehead then stared out the window behind her.

And as they lifted off, he stared down at Skeleton Lake and wondered what the true story was behind the bones riddling the bottom, and whether those who had died in the cave had been punished for what they had done, or were merely innocent victims, whose final resting place should have been this lake of bones.

Approaching Paradise

AD 1255

Three months. It had taken an entire three months for Oldamur's leg to heal and for him to regain enough strength to make the final segment of the journey. He was eager to see his wife and children. Never before had they been separated for so long. His heart ached every day they were apart, but he comforted himself with the knowledge they were already living in the paradise promised to them by Pierre. If it were even half as idyllic as described, it would all have been worth it. The suffering of the journey had been overwhelming at times, but they had all pushed through and deserved the reward that awaited them.

At times, he had wondered if the journey itself were penance, punishment for running away from their problems. He was no fool. He had left problems behind, and they hadn't just disappeared. With his departure, his family had lost its eldest male member. He had abandoned everything in disgrace, a disgrace his family would live with among those they had known all their lives. Two able bodies, and within a few short years, two more, were no longer there to help when it was needed.

No, they had left behind many troubles and created new ones with their departure. Yet he was still certain he had made the right choice, certainly for his wife and children, and perhaps one day, when he was sure they were safe and comfortable, he would make the journey back to make amends. Yet if the ills he had left behind were those of man, he was answerable to God, and if God hadn't wanted him to enjoy this new paradise on Earth, he never would have allowed him to survive for so long. No, he had paid his penance for his sins on this Earth, and saving his mother's soul, and his family from the travails that awaited them back home, were his rewards.

The path curved ahead, and as he rounded it, he gasped at the beauty that lay before him. The land opened up, revealing a lake, crystal blue, the mountains on either side snow-capped, the valley in which he now found himself a lush green. It was stunning, and must be the paradise described by their guide, Pierre.

He quickened his pace, his head on a swivel as he searched for any signs of the others. He heard something behind him and spun, finding several men approaching, something swinging at his head. He raised his hand to block it, but only slowed the blow, the club connecting, excruciating pain following. He collapsed to his knees and held up both hands to protect his head as the next blow rained down on him.

"Father!"

The voice was unmistakable. It was his son, Ajtony.

"Stop!" shouted his daughter. "That's our father!"

Another blow from the club made contact and he cried out in agony as his forearm was shattered. Suddenly his children's hands were on him.

"Father! It was all a lie! They killed Mother! They killed all the parents!" cried his son.

"Stand back!" ordered a voice he recognized immediately. It was Pierre. "Get on your feet."

Oldamur stood with the help of his children, his arm throbbing, his head pounding. He wiped the blood from his eyes and was shocked to see he was surrounded by scores of men, women, and children. Except for Pierre and his son and daughter, he recognized no one. "What's happening here?" he demanded as he struggled to process what was happening. "What have you done with my wife?"

"You would have been proud of her." Pierre stepped closer. "She was the last to die. She fought valiantly, but in the end, she paid the price demanded for her sins. And now, if your God is truly merciful, she is enjoying the Kingdom of Heaven with the others who died that day."

His daughter whimpered and grabbed onto him, his son doing the same. "They killed them all, then they took us and said we were their children now."

Oldamur grasped them with his one good arm. "Why? Why would you do this?"

Pierre ignored him and instead addressed the children. "I need you to step back, children. I need you to keep the promise you made to your new family."

Ajtony shook his head vehemently. "No, I'm staying with my father. He's my family, not you."

Pierre frowned then took a knee in front of Zaleska. "And you, little one, are you going to break your promise like your brother?"

Tears poured down her cheeks. "Yes."

"Very well. You know what happens to those who break the promise."

The two children gripped Oldamur tighter. He glared at Pierre. "What's going on? I demand to know why you've done what you've done."

Pierre regarded him for a moment. "The speech I give, I've already given, and it's meant for the children, not the parents." He turned on his heel and walked away. "Kill them!"

Stones sailed through the air and Oldamur twisted away from the projectiles, shielding his children with his body. He cried out as the first stone hit him squarely in the shoulders, then another and another. Within moments, he was on his knees, agony racking his entire body. A stone smacked his head and his world darkened but he fought back. As he collapsed onto his side, his daughter screamed and she fell beside him, blood trickling from her forehead. As the life drained from the eyes that stared directly into his, he reached for her with his good hand, his own tears flowing now.

They had all been betrayed by a conman who hadn't wanted to save their souls but had instead wanted to steal their children. And it was all his fault. He should never have run away from his problems. He could have fought the Church, and if that had proven unsuccessful, he could have clawed his way back up and rebuilt his life. But instead, he had run, and led his family into tragedy.

His son screamed, his cry cut short as he collapsed atop them. Oldamur reached back to check for any life but found his son's chest horrifyingly still. He was alone now, the last of his family, and he prayed to a God he had never lost faith in, begging that his wife and children, and all those who had paid the ultimate price, be permitted to find peace in Heaven.

And if necessary, to sacrifice his soul to burn for eternity in Hell, a price he would gladly pay for the part he had played in this betrayal.

"That's enough!" ordered Pierre, and the shower of stones abated then stopped.

Footfalls approached but Oldamur was too weak to move. Someone dragged his daughter toward the water, her dead eyes still staring at him. She was followed by his son, then someone grabbed his arms, pulling him toward what was to be his tomb. His broken forearm demanded he respond.

"He's still alive," said the man who had him by the arms. Someone stepped over, stopping beside him.

"Look at me." It was Pierre.

Oldamur forced his eyes open and stared up at pure evil. He spat at him. "You'll burn in Hell for this."

Pierre smiled down at him. "You don't understand. I'm doing the work of God. We all are. We're saving these children, just like we've been saving them for centuries. Everyone you see here was either once a child like your son and daughter, brought here against their will by their parents, or the descendants of such children. We live in peace, knowing we're saving future generations from the corruption of their parents."

"But all you've done is turn them into murderers," gasped Oldamur.

Pierre frowned at him, as if pitying his ignorance. "You'll never understand. You can't understand, because you're one of them, a parent from the corrupt world. Only a child, or someone born here in our peaceful community, could possibly understand." He pointed toward the lake. "Put them over there. You know where. I think he'll enjoy the company."

Pierre turned away and the agonizing drag into the water resumed, and as it deepened, he struggled to keep his head above the surface. But he was too weak, and after several last sputters, he gave up, and instead held his breath for as long as he could as the man continued to drag him before finally letting go. And as he settled on the bottom, and his lungs burned for relief, he turned his head to see his son and daughter beside him. His arm touched something. He turned and a muffled cry erupted at the sight of his wife, her body preserved by the frigid temperature, the horror from her final moments still etched on her face, her eyes wide with her final terror, her mouth agape with her last plea.

Oh, God in Heaven, what have I done?

THE END

ACKNOWLEDGMENTS

I've wanted to write this book since my father sent me a BBC article about Skeleton Lake a couple of years ago. It was a fascinating read, and the research into what they have found, and the theories surrounding it, even more so. Of course, my theory as to what was going on is mine, and comes from a twisted mind I'm proud to call my own.

The China-India conflict was inspired by the outrageous border incident mentioned in the Preface. The image of soldiers battling hand-to-hand literally with sticks and stones in 2020 is simply insane, and the ambush laid by the Chinese where they didn't use guns so they didn't violate any preexisting agreements is something only the twisted mind produced by a lifetime of Communist indoctrination could find reasonable.

Even I could never invent something so ridiculous.

As usual, there are people to thank. My dad for all the research, Brent Richards for some weapons info, Ian Kennedy for some terminology help, and, as always, my wife, my daughter, my late mother who will always be an angel on my shoulder as I write, as well as my friends for their continued support, and my fantastic proofreading team!

To those who have not already done so, please visit my website at www.jrobertkennedy.com, then sign up for the Insider's Club to be notified of new book releases. Your email address will never be shared or sold.

Thank you once again for reading.

Made in United States
North Haven, CT
20 July 2023

39315968R00182